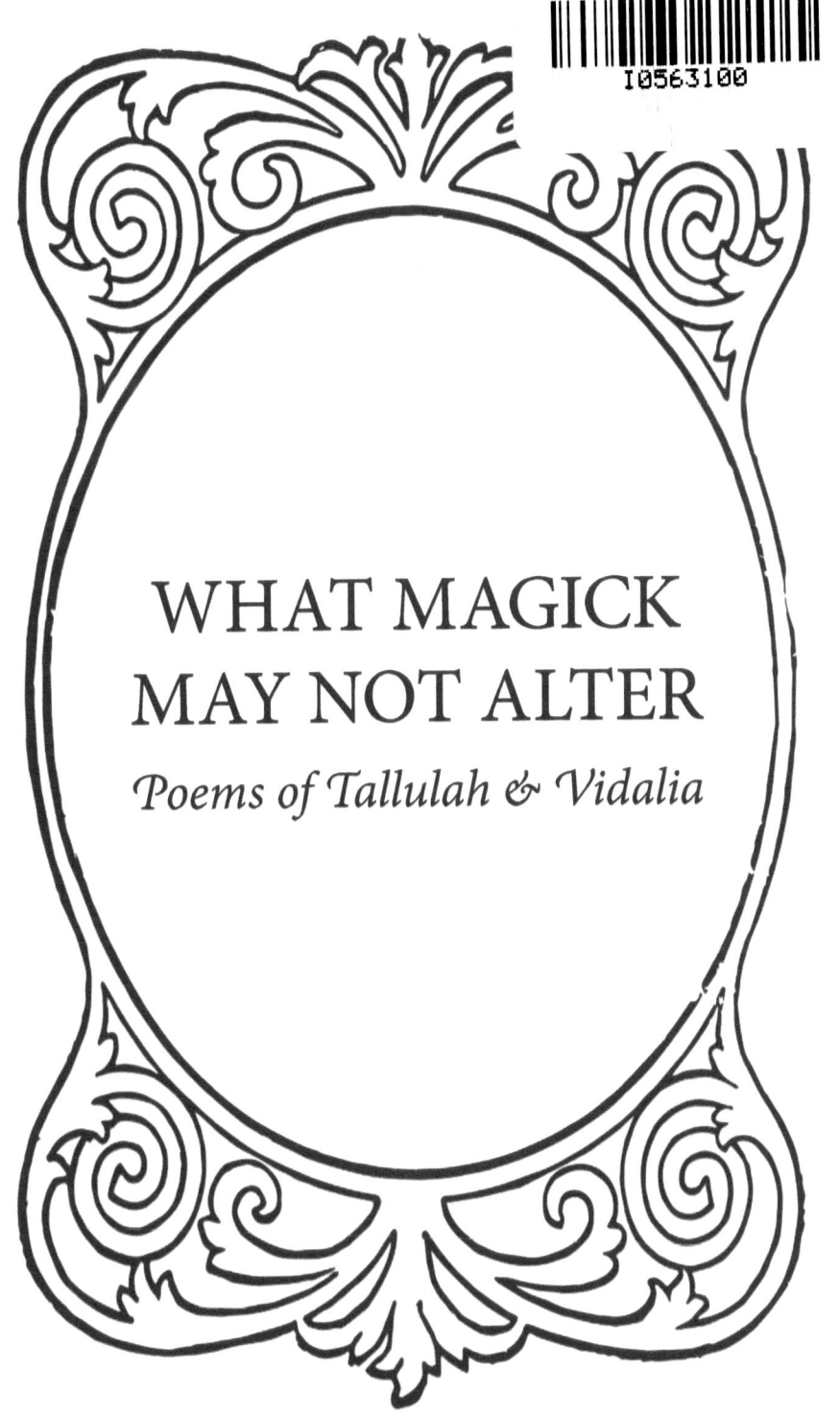

WHAT MAGICK
MAY NOT ALTER
Poems of Tallulah & Vidalia

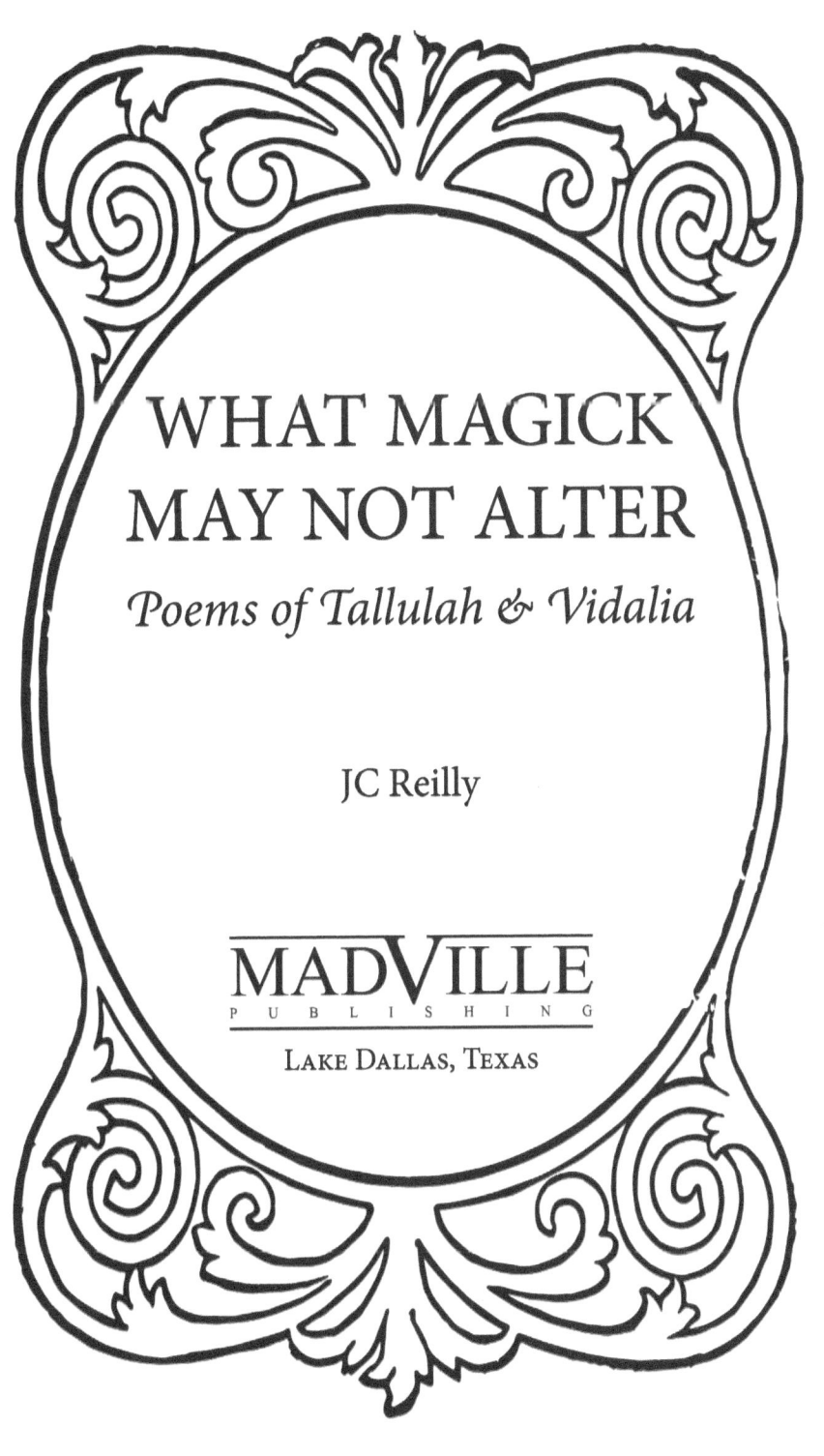

WHAT MAGICK MAY NOT ALTER

Poems of Tallulah & Vidalia

JC Reilly

MADVILLE
PUBLISHING
LAKE DALLAS, TEXAS

FIRST EDITION

Requests for permission to reprint or reuse material from this work should be sent to:

Permissions
Madville Publishing
PO Box 358
Lake Dallas, TX 75065

Acknowledgements:

With grateful thanks to the journals where these poems first appeared, sometimes in altered forms or with different titles:

Arkansas Review:	"They Say," and "Bloom and Doom"
Dead Mule School of Southern Literature:	"Funeral Food and Ida Chatter," "Brittle Moon," "The Colonel's Last Stand," "Bee," "Tallulah Brings Home News"
Fourth & Sycamore:	"Blood Moon," "Hunger Moon," "Hayloft Nativity," "Familiar"
Kentucky Review:	"Contraband," "Beatitude"
Naugatuck River Review:	"Elegy for Cole"
POEM:	"Storm Moon"
Poetry International Online:	"The Three-Hour Siege at the Caddo Parish Jail," "Grannie B Tells the Origin of the Mounds," "A Stop at Old Wives' Oak," "The Invisible Empire on Parade," "ERA at the WDC," "Supplication," "Letter from Tallulah," "Letter from Vidalia," "Unmaking at Old Wives' Oak"
Poetry South:	"Wind Through Corn"
The Poeming Pidgeon:	"Harvest Moon"
South Broadway Ghost Society:	"On the Pier at Hawley Arm, Their Legs Hanging Over the Edge, the Sisters Watch a Storm Punch Its Way from the West"
West Texas Literary Review:	"Caddo Lake Elixir"

Cover Design: Jacqueline Davis
Author Photo: Colin Potts

ISBN: 978-1-948692-30-4 Paper, 978-1-948692-31-1 ebook
Library of Congress Control Number: 2019950587

For my sister, Kirsten

CONTENTS

WHAT MAGICK
MAY NOT ALTER
Poems of Tallulah & Vidalia

I.

The magick in the earth
eats marrow from old bones,
hoards as a blessing
the sparrow in crooked flight.

—Widow Solley

BEE

1.

Grannie Boeuf Sibley's wedding quilt is spread out on their laps, the one Mama should have burned during the Fever, when Grannie's skin turned dulled saffron as the sun behind the smoke from the cotton mill.

2.

Stained from births and deaths, from years of sleeps, its warmth the fabric of memory, the quilt hasn't lain on a bed in years. Too delicate for such utility these days.

3.

The sisters have taken it down from the wall, as if they finally see its age, as if its blemishes seem somehow suddenly to be corrected: the hole in the lavender linsey center star has worsened, and Tallulah eases out the seams of the block, pulling away the cotton batting and the backing with fingers gnarled as crepe myrtles, trying hard not to rub away the fabric like paper.

4.

She takes apart the star as if unmaking the heavens, gives Vidalia the pieces who sets them against tissue to make a pattern for the indigo worsted she has found in a trunk, traces out triangles.

These Vidalia pins to fabric, cuts; begins to sew tiny, even stitches she could make were she blind, hands so used to the in-and-out

advance of the needle, seams straight as compass points.
Star reborn, she returns it to Tallulah who places the block back at
its center, checks for sizing. Vidalia offers the old pieces to stuff into
the batting; not a scrap must be removed, nor history lost. Tallulah
secures the cloth, secrets within a sprig of angelica and thimbleweed,
recreates the stitching of a hundred years past.

The star is not for wishing on.

II.

Sing, sing! Tomorrow
find the reed that whistles
off-tune in the marsh,
hail the bridge that crosses
the chalk stream choked
with watercress.
                    —Widow Solley

Summer Portrait, 1912

In dark suits and matching robin's egg-
washed-gray ties, Benton and Stonewall,
straight-backed as young oaks,
stand on the porch stairs, one behind Mama,
and the other behind Grannie B.

*

Wally, a head taller than Benton
but two years younger, laughs—
at a joke, perhaps, or a dog chasing a squirrel
off-camera. The corners of Benton's mouth
turn up too, but his eyes stray heavenward,
though it's four years until the Seminary.

*

Mama's smile is all-teeth, but not horsey.
How like a Gibson Girl she looks in her new frock,
not unlike when she was married.
The beading on her shirtwaist twinkles
with the sun—and may surely leave faerie flares
on the film. The pleats of her skirt
stay fresh-pressed despite the heat.
She cuddles Rosmerta, then only a kitten,
and doesn't mind the cat hair.

*

Grannie B cocks her head to the left,
her lips twitching as she tries to hold back
a cackle. Twenty years out of date, leg-o-mutton
sleeves on her black bombazine hover like planets
to either side of her, and Cole, sitting on her knee,
seems to fall into their orbit, his wide moon-face
almost dwarfed by their expanse.

*

Magnolia, a little thin,
stands between the elder boys,
her glossy hair drawn back into a bow
the size of angel wings. Freckles dapple
her cheeks prettily, though some of the detail
will be lost in noon sunshine. The twins,
tall for their age and fluffy as meringues
in yards of white, ruffled lawn, hold hands before her.
Vi's heart-shaped face peeps through a curtain
of corkscrew curls, but her expression
is welcoming as an open window.

*

Only Lulah, as if she turned her head
at the last moment, avoids the camera's gaze.
She is smiling too, but at what, she'd never say.

The Three Hour Siege on the Caddo Parish Jail

Shreveport, Louisiana, May 12, 1914

A thousand men had battered
steel doors with railroad irons,
and then hacksawed their way
through the bars, to drag Hamilton
from his cell and tighten a fresh, hemp rope
around his dark thin neck, his screams lost
to the mob's cheers and seething purpose,
his tears erased by May's mid-morning rain.

The Guard never came,
though Sheriff Flournoy telegraphed
the Governor for troops—or so the *Times*
would report the following day,
beside the photograph of the man
the crowds strung up on a telephone pole
across from the Courthouse, caught mid-swing,
Hamilton's head lolling but not snapped,
a trace of foam at his mouth.
The hilt of a knife protruded from his chest
like a key to the door of Hell.

The sisters, not yet ten—
the age of the girl allegedly despoiled—
would not have walked downtown to Dixon's Dry
by themselves, but that Mama's cold
was getting worse, and she needed liniment
and a sack of horehound drops.

They barely made it past
the press of bodies—and the brawls
that spun like eddies in the rush
of angry men on Milam Street—to arrive
at the store, where Mr. Dixon hurried

them inside, locked the door behind them,
let them shelter with the other ladies there.
He led the group in a prayer,
that they wouldn't be burned out,
that the streets would clear, be safe again.
Maybe some of them prayed for the soul
of that Black man—and maybe not.

Years later, of this day, the sisters would not speak.
But more than once, it might be said,
that prayer can't loose the knot
that binds a chiliad of hearts in evil deeds—
and magick has other things to do than try.

THE EQUINOX MOON, MILKY BLUE, DIMS A MOMENT AS PATCHY CLOUDS PASS UNDERNEATH TOWARDS TEXAS

as the sisters sway and sing in
sedgegrass and creeping stickyjack
Grannie B keeps for Restless Tea.

They are too young yet, they're told,
to invoke Ēostre, Blodeuwedd, Demeter—
too young to waken resting earth,

or to dance skyclad with coronets
of meadowsweet in their hair,
or to drink poppy physic brewed

at dawn. Those things come later,
when Moon impels the inner tides
of blossoming women, and when

the circle of mothers opens, and the Gift
becomes theirs. But tonight, promises
and mysteries seem less real

than the ritual of ten-year-olds:
a magick chant they might have dreamed,
a waltz, on tippy-toes, to spring.

FLOWER MOON

Head-to-toe, the sisters form a triangle
in the darkened daisy meadow,
chanting a rhyme Maggie says

is just for little twin girls like them,
not wise yet in magick, but its heir
since the first Sibley sister in Ireland:

> *O Moon of May, O Moon of May*
> *a daisy crown we wear today*
> *to honor Thee, our sacred Queen.*
>
> *Bless us with each bloom we pray*
> *and keep us gentle in Thy ways*
> *till next year when we reconvene,*
>
> *O virgin, mother, crone of May.*

When Grannie calls them in, the Moon dazzles
them home, boon for the novices at their first esbat.

GRANNIE B TELLS THE ORIGIN OF THE MOUNDS

You children been out on the Mounds again,
ain't you? Mercy, all that dirt over your pretty dresses,
and Cole dang near black as your daddy's heart.
Be glad your Mama is out calling on friends,
because I've seen her switch for naughty boys
and girls. Now, don't give me that look, Vidalia!
Heavens, I'm only *teasing* . . . Come to think on it,
your Mama used to climb out here herself
when she wasn't much taller than a cotton bush.
Always said she wanted to find herself some Injun bones,
and don't you think there wasn't some Caddos
to be found. Yes, Cole, *real* Caddo Injuns!
Did you know, there's all kinds of tales how those Mounds
came to be? Some say it was ants. *Ants!* As if
little bitty ants could make fifty-foot circles six feet high!
Some say wind. Others, water volcanoes. Now,
I might not have gone to that fancy St. Vincent's school
for girls like your Mama or your sister Maggie,
(it wasn't built yet, you see, and I suspect
I'd have deviled the nuns), but I'm fairly sure
there's no such thing as a *water volcano*. (Honestly!)
Once, I even heard some folks say the Mounds
were Injun garden-beds piled up to help dry out the soil,
so corn roots wouldn't drown. I could maybe see that . . .
And there *is* bits of Injun pottery turned up all over.
Right here in Stormy Point, back in '85 (your Mama
would've been about ten, then), Col. S. D. Pitts,
a family friend, dug a cellar and uncovered a treasure—
a large pot full of ants (which ain't much of a treasure,
if you ask me). But there was a small pot too, cradling
precious baby bones, as well as keeping rifle barrels,
a knife some eight inches long, and a tomahawk—
which I doubt could *scalp* the dirt of you, Cole—
goodness' sakes, do you have some on your eyelashes? . . .
What was I—oh. Even before then, in 1870

(right before I married Grandpappy, may he rest
Somewhere), high water washed out the southwest corner
of the Point and unearthed a skeleton wearing green copper
shoulder plates and a silver crown. And back then
everyone round here knew the legend of the Last Caddo Chief
buried in the Mounds. —Oh, listen to me! Rambling on
with those same stories I used to tell your Mama and your aunts
and uncles every summer when we'd come up here for a spell
to visit the *beefy* side of the Sibleys. But only your Mama
ever cared much about stories. She still does—kind of like you,
Lulah, in your little scribblings. Alright then, your *verses!*
Now run along, you three, and take off your clothes,
I'll go heat that water for your bath.

CATFISH MOON

Cane poles nearly forgotten beside them,
the sisters scan the lake for ripples.
On this airless August night,

even the moon's reflection in the water
is too sluggish to glint. The yellow cats
aren't biting—though the bait is bream.

They hover close to the cool mud bed.
At this rate, Friday's fish fry won't dish up
more than coleslaw and corn-on-the-cob.

"Maybe not," says Vi, as if Lulah'd spoken
the words aloud. She entreats Selene
from above and Thetis down below, then dips

her hands into the lake, noodling an armful
of flapping cats into an old tin pail.
"They'll call you Jesus, Vi, for this fish tale."

Tallulah Brings Home News

At Dixon's Dry, I was standing
by the sour ball jars and horehound
drops. (I had a nickel, from when I helped
Grannie with the weeding—but I only
planned to spend a penny, honest, Mama.)
Good Christian Mrs. Crockett strolled in,
wrapped in that fox stole she always wears,
even in the heat, and like I wasn't even
standing ahead of her, ordered three yards

of flannel bunting and blue ribbon.
Mr. D brought down the bolt,
shot me a sad ol' sorry look, and asked
what the good word was. Well, you know
she's about as likely to leak a secret
as the Red is to jump its banks after
a gullywasher. Seems that Larasue Buckelew,

who's supposed to marry in the summer,
is pushing up her wedding to Valentine's Day,
as if good Christian folks won't notice her skirts
being let out like circus tents. I said
I thought Valentine's a much sweeter day
to get hitched, 'cause Larasue could wear pink
for her wedding gown and trim it with red
rosettes. But Mrs. Crockett's expression

withered like the watermelon vines behind
Grannie's barn, said there's only *one* reason
a girl won't wear white, and wasn't it
a shame, a scandal, an abomination
in a good Christian family? Why,
Larasue was lucky she wasn't being sent away
to the Sisters, and she's a *Baptist*. Mrs. Crockett
made us swear we wouldn't tell just as Mr. D

finished cutting the cloth and wrapping it
in butcher paper. He wouldn't gossip
anyhow—those Dixons are quiet as river
stones—and I said if I spoke a word of it
the Lord should smite me where I stand.
That's why I stopped at Holy Trinity on the way
and pre-confessed my loose tongue.
God can't do a *thing* to me now.

A Stop at Old Wives' Oak

Its leaves have turned coal-orange
and brown as cinnamon crisp,
and Maggie is late in planting
her one, her true, her daffodil—the wispy
bulb paper crinkling

in the yawn of afternoon breeze.
She's sworn the twins, just-turned-teen,
to secrecy, as she scoops a hole
in the earth, then sets the bulb like a queenly
diadem in its cache—and polls

for their opinion. Lulah snorts
cicada-sharp, goes back to her whittling,
but Vidalia softens like a lemon cream,
a dream of romance (and her teeth) nibbling
at her lip. "It's perfect." She beams

at her elder sister, and Maggie smooths
the last of the dirt on top, says a spell
for winter to be kind, and spring
to be kinder yet. *May what dwells
here now in warmer months bring*

felicity, she thinks. As for sisters
sowing wishes, how far off *some day* seems—
Maggie envisions that yellow bloom, thick
with promise. The Oak gleams
bright fire, shakes off its leaves like magick.

Cold Moon

Midwinter nights are longest now,
and your arc across the sky
(opposite the low, cold sun)

is fixed and leisurely and high
above the horizon—as if twins
who mark the hours till Yule

don't chafe to plot your tortoise
path and wish to magick up a spell
to make the hands of clocks spin fast,

sink you again beneath the world,
and hasten treasures
of the day, bright silver-twirled

and golden-bowed, to them.
But in fullness, you condemn
hearts, still, to dream of Bethlehem.

III.

What you have said
becomes the pear that in sorrow
lays down its leaves
like the faces of unborn pigs.

—Widow Solley

They Say

Plant a daffodil at Old Wives' Oak:
you will meet your future
husband on the day it blooms.

Early spring, the ground boasts
an orchestra of trumpets,
the wishes of other brides,
pushing up between yawns
of yellow grass—

Even Mama—
never one for folklore
    and doubtful

        Narcissus

             could conjure
a husband worth a damn—

found herself down on her knees,
digging a hole,
for bulbs called "Lovejoy"
    and   "Aflame."

If Grannie B said
it was high time she put her linens in order,
could Mama do otherwise?

Two years later,
she'd marry Delhi.

    But she'd seen his brother Cavett too,

        that February day

           she and Daddy met

and hoped the right bloom
had opened first.

Vidalia Casts for a Soul Mate

I. *Inventory the Attributes*
My list, O Áine, is not long.
Let his call to me be *you-oo-oo.*
Let him beckon with a noisy flight
of laughter; in the quiet hours,
with a flap of his soft blond
hair. Let his constancy run
deep as those black bead eyes.

II. *Ready the Elements*
Bright with opportunity,
the waxing moon hangs like a medal
on the breast of the sky.

On this cypress stump, my altar:

>   *rose petals,*
>   *a snip of sage for purity's sake,*
>   *a Valentine,*
>   *a small copper brazier,*
>   *a candle from our beeswax store,*
>   *the list I've penned on linen rag.*

Beneath me, the ground, seething
with drought, cools.

And fire—
I touch paper to flames,
release the burning to copper. Words
curl in on themselves, lift into the universe
on lashes of smoke.

III. *Entreat the Goddess*
Áine, bring forth this true and loving man:
So mote it be. So mote it be.

ELEGY FOR COLE

Mama's cat would have come down eventually—
when she got hungry, when she got tired.
We all said so. You were so proud,
as you scuttled up the Colonel's trunk
like a Lou'siana black bear and inched
your way out on that gangly branch
not much thicker than a broomstick
where Rosmerta sat trembling, yowling,
the crow she'd chased long flown off.

We could not hear soft words you spoke,
but something of a Sibley lilt charmed
the yowls to mews and then to quiet
watchfulness. When you scooped her
into your arms the way a bear grabs at fish
over a waterfall, she might have panicked.
But she settled over your left shoulder
like a sack of sugar, and you scooted
your way back towards the trunk,
using your right hand for balance.

The crack, when it came, seemed almost off-hand,
lazy and loud as a bear yawn.
You kept the cat close, your arm tourniquet-
tight, even as her nails must have pierced
your flesh, even as your own nails dug
vainly into bark, and caught only air
for thirty feet, missing lower branches
as if magick miscalculated to slow descent.
We scrambled beneath the Colonel,
thought softer bodies could ease your impact.

At ten feet, Rosmerta lept free, and though
you landed mostly on top of us, the back
of your head found the only axe-sharp

rock jutting from the soil. So hard
were we laughing you were saved,
we overlooked it till we stood you up.
You wobbled, cried out, and pitched
forward into Vidalia, and we saw: blood,
blood, and shattered bone matting
brown curls over a rift in your skull
deep as Southern honor. Maggie raced to get
Mama and Grannie B, a spell to stanch
the bleeding. But you were dead.

That night in the sky, Ursa Minor glowed
unusually bright, and we knew
the heavens had already made you their own.

Funeral Food and Ida Chatter

Grannie B and the Widow step out from the parlor
full of mourners onto the front porch, each carrying
a glass of sweet tea and a plate piled high with funeral food.

As they sit in the swing, Grannie says, "If we have to gnash
our teeth over the death of my grandson, we may as well
gnash our teeth on Florien Crockett's fried chicken."

"Lordy, Ida, be nice!" says the Widow. She picks up a drumstick
and bites into it. "Is that *Tabasco* I taste? And cinnamon?"
"Anything's possible," says Grannie, glancing at the chicken.

She shoots a dubious look at the rest of the plate's contents:
tuna casserole, tuna-broccoli-noodle casserole, coleslaw,
broccoli-rice casserole, pork-n-beans, ten layer salad,

potato-bacon-cheese casserole à la Someone-or-Other
from the Church, dumplins, and pineapple upside-down cake.
"Heaven knows, the best thing to do when someone dies

is *eat*." Grannie's laugh is cold as Caddo Lake in January,
and sharp as the swing's creak. She says, "Goldie ain't stopped
crying since his fall." The Widow puts a free arm around her.

"Let's do a healing tonight," she invites. "I have new sage."
Grannie nods as she pushes her food around. It makes a face,
a Medusa perhaps, but not good enough a likeness to turn

her to stone, though she might wish it could. She shoves
the plate behind her on the railing. She doesn't turn her head
at the noise when it crashes to the porch. "It's Delhi all over,

trying to catch that twenty he won at cards that blew out
of his pocket and over the side of the KCS bridge.
He had about as much sense as a coin purse after tax day.

And Cole's just like his dad. Why, he wouldn't know bright
if Edison handed him a lightbulb." She might have said more,
but thinks better of it as Mama shuffles out on the porch

looking as if she's fallen into a well of loneliness and soaked
through with tears. Not that Grannie minds talking ill of the dead,
just not where polite folks—and grieving mothers—can hear.

Confessional

I think I saw Miss Vi-and-mighty
stuff a couple of Mama's best handkerchiefs
in her underthings when she dressed this morning.

She'd give Narcissus a run for his money
always preening in the mirror,
patting at her hair twisted up in some squirrel's nest
of a knot. A pair of braids was plenty fine

a month ago. And those long skirts
and silky blouses with pearl buttons
may be hand-me-downs from Mama's friend
but they're still too fancy for the likes of her—
a chicken in peacock feathers.

I've even heard her murmur to Magnolia
about hope chests and linens and wedding balls
held at Hotel Youree, and *two* sisters
talking such pig-slop is more than I can take.

I swear, if she makes plans to plant daffodils
at Old Wives' Oak, I'll sock her straight in the eye,
and I don't much care if I get a hiding for it.

Rainy Afternoon

"A disgrace to Sibley women everywhere,"
Lulah sighs. She couldn't even magick
a straight stitch if she wanted to—sometimes,
being the unGifted sister held more drawbacks
than she cared to count. "I don't know why
Vi said she wanted us to make this quilt

for Mama anyway. She sure hasn't worked
a lick on it." Thunder cracks, and she feels
it straight to her heart—and something darker
she can't name settles like a cold, dripping hand
about her shoulders. That Vi! Courting left

no time for anything, like these more *useful*
feminine arts. Thank goodness for Maggie.
As her sister re-stitches the heart, Lulah picks up
a kitten and nuzzles its bright gray nose.
Kittens aren't magick but they sure come close.

Bloom and Doom

Before the first web of frost,
before the ground
could rebuke such offerings,

I settled my bulb in the earth
where the roots of Old Wives' Oak
form three heart-shaped knots.

With a fallen twig, I scratched
"BF" into its papery husk.
Lulah would chide me for a cheat,

but I wished to nudge Gaia
or Balanos or the spirits of wives past
to ensure I'd encounter my one true love.

Through months of somber rains
and fish-cold winds, I waited
for the green tip to peep

through red clay, its promise near.
I charted its growth
a hundredth of, a tenth of, half an inch,

mindful not to tread on young green hopes
of sister brides, as I set my measure
beside the stalk. For weeks now

I've kept this vigil, watching yellow
flutter and bounce as other stalks
unsheathed pale heads, noted

the pink-cheeked girls who've come
to check heights against their own rulers.
Already some blooms begin to droop,

and still mine stays tight within its sepals,
like pursed lips, a kiss denied,
a husband who won't come when you call.

The Colonel's Last Stand

Too wet a spring
has made Caddo swallow
its shoreline like a tide too set
in its ways to roll back out,
the hard Lou'siana clay
boggy, its sandbars a myth.

Even what's not lake officially
sucks boots up to the calves:
Hawley Arm less land than sponge.
Grannie B says at this rate
she'll have to row the *Brittle Moon*
past the barn to check the melons.

Today, what she calls
a "Southern drizzle": bladder-sized
splatters to drown you where you stand—
unless you're one of the cypresses,
which haven't the sense to mind
the water creeping up their trunks
like hemlines on a Flapper.

Not so this sage magnolia,
which minds too much—the magnolia
dubbed "the Colonel" after her Papa,
planted on a rise overlooking
the lake when her parents wed,
before the War—back when everything,
including the lake, knew its place.

And then—a waver of limbs,
soundless with the storm-whipped
water—the magnolia eases
sideways, slides into the lake to lie
half-submerged, a strange counterfeit

to the cypresses. Muddy roots
pulled free push wildly at the air,
like bones in a mass grave, dug up.

Grannie B takes in the fallen tree
from the porch. "It's too wet
to cry over the Colonel. Lord knows,
we did enough of that at Mansfield."

In the lake, filled to the brim,
white teacup blooms on wide green saucers.

Blue Moon

The third in a season with four,
or the second to show in a month?
The almanac, for planting times,

asserts a season's extra moon as blue,
while folklore—and Grannie—say
twice in a month is true. This *blue*

comes to us from *belewe,* Old English
belǽwian, to betray; and *betray* derives
from Latin *traděre,* to hand over,

so the Blue Moon is Judas' Moon:
the Old Church would grieve its arrival
in Lent as The Betrayer. In 1901,

the moon is bluest the last of July,
when, cut from his mother's moon belly,
the eldest Ferry, that rough beast, breathes air.

HAYLOFT NATIVITY

Figaro, more fleas than cat, sits
on the planks she poached from Dixon's Dry
that form this desk across the bales.
He starts to groom the star
of his bottom just as she sets down the bag.
She tucks her skirt beneath her
on the seat, its horse-blanket cover
not quite keeping her from being stuck,
and prepares the scene,

mindful of Figgy: she brushes stray
flecks of hay to the floor, pulls out
a battered notebook, nearly empty,
an almost-new bottle of ink,
and the Colonel's silver pen.
She dips the nib into the ink, black
sucking up in channels thin as eyelashes,
presses it to that first page—

where there are other such spots,
the ink veining spiders of hesitation.
What she could write: lists of notions,
quilt patterns, recipes copied from a card,
letters to the *Times*, accounts
of seeding or the honey harvest,
detailed blueprints for revenge—
or what *sings*, though it's secret, secret:

those rhymes
that river through her thoughts
when common tasks should keep her care.
But today, she pushes beyond
those first falterings,
cuddles close the infant lines.

Old Wives' Oak, Again

The daffodils bloomed early
that year—the end of January—
before the rabbits left their warrens,

before the mice crept from their nests,
before I knew to pluck a sister's hope:
this flower that should have stayed

numb in the ground, to rot
in its sheath, the way the one for whom
she'd planted it should lie in pine and satin

by mirror hands. But I arrived too late:
she, at her daily vigil, marking,
measuring, praying, had seen him

saunter by, the collar on his jacket
turned up against the wind, the flush
in his cheeks she'd always find

endearing, which even then was gin's,
not winter's, doing. I could not spare
her, once the Old Wives' magick

struck; as dumb love clouded her eyes,
fate's yellow trumpet resounded
through somber-bare branches, like a sigh.

BONHAM FERRY COMES TO CALL

Look at him, spread out on Grannie B's
swansdown settee like rancid butter on a biscuit,
with that bouquet of snapdragons
he snitched from the Widow's yard.

You'd think Vi'd see right through him,
with his pomaded hair, that smirk wide
as his lapels, the way he hisses all his *S's*
like a lisping cottonmouth. But she and Mama
are snowed as the Arctic. It's always
"Bonham this" and "Bonham that,"
and "Isn't he such a fine young man?"
If he's so upright, why does it seem
like everything I know about him is slanted?

I've *heard* things.
Oh, that he's been seen at the cathouses
in St. Paul's Bottoms, owes people money,
that a Creole girl on Fannin Street's
gone missing, and the last person seen
with her was a blond boy in a Cadillac Model S.

I can't *prove* anything,
but even once in a while the aspersions
Mrs. Crockett casts on Shreveport's Elite
(when she's buying supplies and running
her mouth off at Dixon's) ring just a little
truer than the rest. And he *does* flash
that Caddie around. But there's no repeating
this to Vi. She wouldn't believe
those rumors anyhow.

That's why I've kept my mouth shut
so far, but if Vidalia's setting
her cap for the likes of him,

only heartache can come of it,
and no amount of moony incantations
and goddess invocations will set things aright.
He's a bad, bad man, and we'll all be sorry.

I'd like to take that bottle of hooch
poking out of his coat pocket
and dump it right over his greasy ol' head,
but Grannie B's asked me to serve him lemonade.
Oh, were it strychnine instead.

COURT REPORTER

To hear Grannie B and Mama talk,
my sister's wedding is any day.
What else are they to think,
with Bonham calling on her yet again?
Even Vidalia's lost count
how many afternoons she's kept
his company, and she writes down
everything in that old diary she keeps.

Mama shouldn't allow these visits—
and wouldn't, if she knew, as I do,
that Bonham *never* once has spoken
of such a thing. All she and Grannie see
is how they look a picture in our swing:
Vidalia in pincurls beneath her cloche,
and comely as a daffodil in the yellow,
beaded dress she finished last night,
and him in fresh seersucker,
holding her hand as if it were a dove.

She'll tell me tonight they discussed
the heat, or baseball, or church,
or his new job at the freight yard,
while she glances forlornly at her hand
and twists an imaginary ring.
She'll say he has to make his way
before she can set her linens in order,
and really, isn't she a *ninny*
to be so impatient?

I'll listen to her, as I always do, whispering
it won't be long till he declares
himself. But I hold the hope
that his delay will outlive his suit.

Letter from Pvt. Stonewall Sibley Winnsboro

Alexandria, Louisiana, October 1918

Dear Mama—
By now you know I've run off to Camp Beauregard
to join the 39th Infantry. They say we'll all deploy to France
at some point, but most of us here—men in the best shape
of their lives—is sick as two dogs. Earlier, it was measles
or meningitis, now it's Spanish flu and pneumonia.
(It's pande-pneumoni-um as we call it.) I spent six days
puking up my guts—pardon, Mama—and had chills
and a fever of 102 from flu. Soon as I felt some better,
Captain give me a choice: latrine duty, or helping the nurses.
Ain't no way I was going to clean those stinkholes
full time with all that dysentery and flu floating around
(though most times, soldiers can't hold their bowels
till they get to the latrines—sorry, Mama). Anyway,
the medics was running out of room in the field hospitals,
and leaving soldiers on cots just out in the air to spread
disease to those who ain't caught it yet. A pretty nurse
told me to keep the soldiers comfortable, with cold rags
on their heads, and just to give them a lot of aspirin
(because we didn't have nothing else, really) to bring down
the fevers. All that aspirin seemed to make some die quicker,
though, if you ask me, but I give it to them.
                                                            Sometimes,
when the soldiers' delirium clears up, but they're still too sick
to train, I write letters home for them, telling their families
that they're doing well, and that they're looking forward
to helping the Froggies whip them Krauts good. I even wrote
a couple marriage proposals to the men's sweethearts,
though one Cpl. died the next day 'cause his lungs was so full
of fluid he drowned. I wished I hadn't already put that letter
in the post, but it was too late to get it back. I plumb hate
thinking about some girl's broken heart. I dallied with writing
her another letter, telling her he'd changed his mind,

and that he didn't love her—that way when she gets
the notification she'll be too mad about the phony proposal
to be sad he's gone on to his reward, but I figured best not to meddle.
(Maybe you and those sisters of mine can conjure up a charm
for her. And if not, then maybe some prayer would work.)

Anyway, don't be mad at me, Mama, for enlisting.
I may have been too young to draft, but I ain't too young
to fight for God and country.

—Your loving son, Wally

As Ye Have Done Unto the Least of These

Before they see the inky clot
flailing in the road, they hear the puppy's
strangled yelps and whimpers.
Vidalia starts to pray, to run
the Highland Park stop,

where the puppy has snared a paw
in a cleft between pavement and rail.
Always on time, the street car
will arrive at two minutes past,
but she bends low, cradles its face,

whispers nonsense words
and pleas to St. Francis and Artemis,
while Bonham catches up, cursing
damn curs and half-wit women
with their jelly-soft hearts.

The puppy trembles as she pries
at cobblestone, works to coax
the paw, damp with a paste
of blood and dirt, from its trap.
The streetcar rounds the corner

at Highland and Olive. From the sidewalk,
Bonham bellows at her to let
the damn thing die, but still she keeps
whispering, her voice urgent, soothing,
promising freedom, glad the advancing

beams leak enough light into the crevice
that she can discern how the paw
has twisted under the metal,
and just as the street car clangs
its arrival, she thrusts the paw under

and up, grabs the puppy in her arms,
jumps to safety, only the sweep of her skirts
struck. Everyone is shouting then—
the driver, the passengers, Bonham—
all noise, all, to the puppy's eager kisses.

THE FOUR HORSEMEN OF THE APOCALYPSE

Finding him every bit as handsome
as Valentino, if not so dark and Latin,
she kisses him as they emerge
from Saenger Theatre, the lights
from the marquee making
something of a halo around him.

Ushers in red and gold
hold the doors as movie-goers
spill out to either side of them.
She doesn't pay attention, though—
lost, as she is, in Buenos Aires tonight.

She smiles to imagine him clad
in *bombachas*, and the black, stiff
sombrero with the four pom-poms.
Her arms, more slender
than a leather *rastra*, cinch tight at his waist.
The cigarette hangs already from his lip.

"Would you cut in if I tangoed
with another man? Would you strike
him, and take me in your arms? Would you
kiss me when our dance was through?"
Her heart gives a leap as she awaits his *yes*.

He looks down at her, his eyes
bulging dramatically as Valentino's
when the tango dancers took the floor—
and again before the silent star
struck his rival who dared refuse him
the beauty in flowers and fringe.
Her heart leaps again.

"If you tangled with another man,
he wouldn't be the only one beat
with a bat and sent sprawling into tables."

At her quick gasp,
he laughs, and tweaks her nose.
She laughs too—a little.
What are war and famine, pestilence and death,
next to a few bruising words from him?

ASHES, WEDNESDAY

Before she turns to undress,
I glimpse something batlike
round her eye, darker than the smudge
still visible on her forehead
from Church this morning.
She does not speak, and when I move
to place my hand on her shoulder,
she flinches, scuttles under the blankets
like a thin, spooked cat,
and curls towards the wall.

I creep downstairs to the kitchen.
From Grannie's herb pantry,
a few things—a philter of arnica oil,
feverfew for tea. As the water boils,
I crush calendula petals with a pestle,
fold them into some cheesecloth
that I wrap around a hunk of ice,
whisper almost without thought

> *On your face his menace clings,*
> *a livid brown, this darkness stings.*
> *Tomorrow may fairer glance prevail:*
> *the swelling gone—a heart that sings.*

I pour the water over the tea, add sugar,
gather remedies on a tray.

Upstairs again, I sit beside Vi,
pull her gently toward me.
She does not resist this time, lets me
apply the arnica with faerie touch,
its pine-sagey scent easing both her and me.

Her lips, ashy, accept my quick kiss.
I give her the calendula compress,
urge her to drink some tea.

How much longer till what must be?

BRITTLE MOON

Three quarters' full: Vi in the back seat;
Lulah, center, rowing; Honey in the prow
barking at clouds and pelicans on derricks.

Cypress stumps stretch across the surface
like a hall of empty seats. It's not quite nine.
The bass and crappie might be biting.

In reeds, they stop and bait their hooks with red-
and-butterworms. Vi whispers half-a-spell
to make hers work harder; it shimmies on cue.

The only thing Lulah casts is her line—
and muttered slanders against Vi's taste in beaux.
Honey settles in to snooze. As Saturday morning

darkens into noon, Lulah's scowl seems to break
the weather: Vi's ease fades, a mist in the squall;
the fish like phantoms in the empty hall.

Spring Training

Shreveport, Louisiana, March 12, 1921

Leaping to their feet,
Bonham, Calvin, and Stonewall
chant along with the crowd,
Home Run! Home Run!
Vi and Maggie rise politely
beside their beaux, while Lulah stands
on her seat, bracing against her brother,
to see past Bonham's greasy head.

There he is! Babe the Mighty!
He struts from the dugout,
extends a southpaw wave to 4,000 fans,
and picks up two bats, as if weighing
which will send the horsehide
further over the fence of Gasser Park.

He tosses one aside, steps into the batter's box,
waits for Watson's windup and release—
Ruth windmills, but the ball powers
into Greenase's mitt. *Strike one!*

At Watson's smalltown heater, he smirks,
Is that all you got? The big boy swings—
spins clean off his feet, and lands
on his red-clay-dusty keister. *Strike two!*

Watson's last pitch, too low
and slow for the Bambino to pay it
much notice, dawdles over the plate
like Grannie B on her way home from church.
Strike three! Yerrrrrrrrrrrout!

The fellas slump down in the bleachers
and groan like they've eaten too much
cotton candy and Crackerjacks.
The rest of the crowd groans too.
The fence—and fans—have to hope
another inning will let fly
the Sultan's homerun voodoo.

Lulah pounds a fist in the air and shouts,
"Get your eyes checked, Moriarty!
Anyone can see the ball was polishing
his shoes! Why, your strike zone's
the size of Bossier City!"

Vi rolls her eyes, and Maggie, worried
what Calvin must think, shushes her.
But Lulah continues to heckle the ump
till Moriarty flicks off his mask.
It flaps in his hand like a mad crow.
"Listen, Sister, you put a sock in it
or *yerrrrrrrouttahere* too!"
Wally knuckleballs her mouth full
of popcorn before she can respond.

About to leave the plate, Ruth scans
the crowd to see who started
the racket. Spotting Lulah still tall
on her seat, he flourishes his cap, and bows.
The crowd cheers, half-heartedly,
as he wanders back to the dugout.
Even a legend isn't a legend all the time.

FAMILIAR

Her sisters have spent the better part
of Saturday preparing
for the Sodality Spring Dance,
while Lulah, in overalls, hides in the hayloft
with her notebook and her pen,
trying out some new lines
that will never sound like those she's read
in *Michael Robartes and the Dancer*.
What does she know of uprisings
and apocalypse?

At her feet, the latest batch of barncats—
more anarchy loosed upon the world—
bask in an old horse blanket
and some flannel bunting.
Proud papa Figgy, an arc of smoke,
stretches beside Rosmerta as she nurses
four torties and a nimbus-colored male
Lulah's already nicknamed Chance—
short for Cloudy with a Chance.

Their small squeaks and purrs
distract a moment from words
that come sludge-dull and slow,
and from the sting of sister-sympathy.

Oh—but if he'd asked,
would some kind of magick be at hand?
Would Sibley magick be at hand?
Likely—and Lulah would have turned
any young man down,
just in case his will was coaxed.

She bends to tickle Chance's belly,
the vapor-soft fur almost a revelation.

He looks at her, his topaz eyes
bright sunlight streaking through a thunderhead.
Another revelation—that his will
might be coaxed by *her*—

I am yours, written as if automatically,
on a fresh page in her book.

THE INVISIBLE EMPIRE ON PARADE

No horns, but pipes and drums resound
unimpeded by ghostly drapery
as the Knights of the Bayou parade
downtown. Six men abreast
carry the Stars and Bars, and another six,
a pennant with bright red lettering,
Shreveport Klan #2 Wants You.
The pageant in white extends as far down
McNeill Street as the sisters can see.

At the edges, a few men break formation
to give sweets to small children,
or to salute amputees back from war,
or to pass out pamphlets and "Do You Know" cards.
One is slipped into Tallulah's hand.
She whispers, "This here says Pope Benedict XV
is hell-bent on taking over America.
I don't think he can be bothered, myself."
Vi whispers back, "We shouldn't be here."

Next to her, Bonham claps and cheers
along with the crowd. He turns to Vi,
slaps her slight shoulders in a hug.
"I'm signing up at the picnic afterwards."
"Idiot boy, you're a *Catholic*," says Lulah.
Several looks are shot their way,
the only things dark about the faces nearby.
Bonham appears as though he might reply,
then crushes Vi a little closer to him.
Her whimper is almost lost in a martial surge
of voices singing "The Old Rugged Cross."

The Knights turn east along Texas Street,
towards the river and the picnic promised
at parade's end. Disgust—at Bonham,

at white robes hiding craven hearts,
at sweet, spineless Vi—wells up in Lulah then,
hot and sudden as a burning cross.

Loaded Down with Sugar and Rice for Mama and Quilting Swatches for Vi, I Run Smack Dab into That Unctuous Bonham Ferry

"Hello, Ta-loooooooo-lah," he hoots
like a barn owl. "How's that fetching sis
of yours?" He takes a low bow,
and I wonder that the pomade
in his hair don't slide off
and smear the planks of the stairs.

"Fetching as ever." I side-step
as he straightens up, to be on my way.
But he oils along like a Texas gusher
in stride beside me.
"Let me take those," he says, sliding
the parcels out of my hands.
"A delicate *fleur* like you
shouldn't have to carry all that."

I'd say no, and probably
sock him for good measure,
but I notice that old gossip Mrs. Crockett
and Cora Pearl, the cotillion-queen,
approach, and Mama won't be too keen
if I make a hoyden of myself—
well, more than she says I am already.
(Propriety being next to Godliness with her.)

So he walks me home, oozing
charm, his compliments
to me, to Mama, to Vi, hot bacon greasy
as Grannie B's Sunday breakfast,
and not nearly as easy on the gullet.

When we arrive, Vidalia emerges
from the garden like Pomona,

bearing apples. The packages
dropped in a heap, Bonham turns
to her. All I can think is oh,
how gifts of grace forgotten,
he'll slick his Vidalia ere he eats her.

Caddo Lake Elixir

Vidalia tethers the *Brittle Moon*
to a thick cypress on the Texas side
of Tar Island Slough, while I nurse
my hands from the paddles' chafing.

It didn't seem so far from Hawley Arm
when we set out after supper,
but half-a-mile's rowing
has brought out the mosquitoes,
and the sky sinking to purple
casts its reproach along with the shadows:

it's more than a mile around the island,
and there might be gators—
worries too mundane for Vidalia's magick,
but not for me. To navigate by starlight
might work for sea captains,
but I have neither sextant nor compass
to guide our voyage back, and hope
someone turns on the lantern at the pier.

Undaunted, she opens her satchel,
draws out a beeswax candle, cardamom,
clove, and damiana leaves. She lights
the candle on the seat beside her, scoops
some lake water in a bowl, tosses in the herbs.
This she heats above the flame a few minutes,
whispers words too soft to be heard
over the bullfrogs and cicadas, then sips.

If she twists up her face like a dish towel
at the taste, I don't see it, but feel my own
wrinkle in sympathy. "So mote it be,"
she says, pouring the rest back into the lake,
and blowing out the candle whose smoke

threads its way unseen into the fabric
of the evening. "We can go."

She unties the boat from the tree
and pushes us back into the channel.
As the paddles cut through the slough, a hint
of clove catches on the breeze like grace.

Pink Moon

The moss pinks that creep
wild in meadows and along the house
at Hawley Arm give you your name.

Though you are white as ever
against April's impudent darkness,
your veil upon the pinks—

and her, your votary—gleams
like bone, like the ruffled edge of the queen
conch she found at Grand Isle

four summers ago, like snail paths
on sidewalks, like ghost-frosted breath.
Their petals, notched hearts, reach

for you in swaying aves. Hers, a deeper red,
she lifts towards you in entreaty,
implores too much, for love.

ERA AT THE WDC

Today's meeting of the Women's Department Club
buzzes with ladies, and a few husbands
more or less tied to their wives by sashes
or buttons proclaiming Equal Rights for All
sit quietly bored. Guests drink tea or nibble
petite water chestnut sandwiches on marble bread,
though Lulah spits hers into a handkerchief,
"These taste like sheep *sh*—a sheep's pen."
The remark earns her a shove from Vi
and cherry-sour looks from Maggie and Mama.

With a Baptist preacher's fervor,
the Club president orates an article
reprinted from Monday's *New York Times*.
She punctuates the text with asides and angry smacks
to the podium, seething over Samuel Gompers'
backhanded concern for women's safety:
> *"The difference of opinion is over the question*
> *of whether the proposed blanket amendment would result*
> *in the destruction of standards and safeguards*
> *now established in the law of the States*
> *for the protection of women in industry . . .*
> *I assure the women of the country that those laws*
> *would be not only endangered but would be destroyed."*
She stamps her foot at that pronouncement, and adds,
"Ladies, that . . . that *Jew Communist* wants to protect us
right out of our rights, the same way our great State of Louisiana
refuses to ratify the 19th Amendment—over a year
after the men in Washington have ratified it
for the entire country. *We must not stand for it.*"
Lulah whispers, "He's not even a Socialist, you know."
"Be quiet," Vi hisses.

The president finishes reading, then introduces
a Shreveport attorney, John D. Williams, one of four Southern men

the *Times* mentions to endorse the National Women's Party
campaign. His speech whips up a crowd already frothy,
and when he concludes, even the husbands stand to clap.
Mama, who never says much, looks positively lovesick,
as she glides from her seat to the front of the room
to shake his hand and thank him for his words.

Maggie and Vi swoon a bit as well, but Lulah says,
"Don't see why we have to depend on men
to give us women's rights . . . Couldn't magick fix this?"
Maggie's sigh rolls out like mist. "You know it can't."
No, of course not—magick only bends the will of one.
There are still too many men to be undone.

Wind Through Corn

As Lulah comes to a clearing in the maze,
and stares overhead at horse white clouds
galloping across a too-blue-for-October sky,
the wind shaking the Gold Queen leaves
like a thousand rattlers blows a kernel
of truth her way: that she can't be lost,
not she who draws earth energy
through her feet to her heart to her lungs,
and releases it back to creation
with breath and thanks
as every Sibley woman before her has done.

She breaks off a cob, peels away the floss,
and tosses it free. It glints like a flame,
like a faerie on a fresh burst of wind—
flying eastward, towards exit, towards home.

BUCK MOON

On the bush and bramble side
that fringes toward the wood,
a whitetail stag sniffs the air

then lowers its tongue to Caddo's
edge to drink. Under your watch,
its eight points gleam a dull,

milky opal, and catch in cattail
cluster. With a quick head shake,
and a nose blow nearly laugh-like,

it frees its antlers. Another sip; the deer
finishes its lake water nightcap.
As it clops off into the loblollies,

alert but unhurried, you darken
to think of hunters, sleeping now,
dreaming all of Actaeon's fate.

Their Boots Kick Up Dust that Hems Their Skirts with a Dingy Ribbon

"It doesn't feel much like October,"
says Vidalia, fanning herself
with a letter they're sending
to Benton, with nine dollars they raised
for his Manzanillo mission
and "those blessed, poor Indians."

They stop at Dixon's Dry
where the "good" post box sits,
the ones hooligans won't mess with,
since Old Papi rocks in his chair
in front of the store, a pipe in one hand,
his Colt 1851 in the other.

"Mornin', Ladies," Old Papi says,
"What you got there?" Vi drops
the letter in the box, then pauses
to chat with the old soldier, her smile
gardenia-fresh despite the heat,
while Lulah slips inside to find

a bottle of ink and a blank notebook.
Mr. Dixon, reading the *Times*,
looks up and asks, "May I . . . ?"
But Lulah, beside the stationery display,
waves him off. "I'll find something,"
she assures him. "What news is there?"

> *Another Bottoms girl gone missing,*
> *and cotton prices down. A fire*
> *in Broadmoor, the Lt. Governor in town,*
> *the ground-breaking on the Strand,*
> *a Knights of the Bayou social planned—*

"Just another day in Shreveport," he says.

Vi comes in then to collect her,
as Mr. Dixon rings her up. The sisters
nod to Old Papi and start back home.
"What did you buy for two bits?" asks Vi.
Lulah considers, dabs sweat from her brow.
"A poem about Fall," she says.

IV.

Stanch the blood, O yarrow,
from wounds of war;
hurry the blood of the young girl,
whose belly clenches
with fever and burning
womanhood.

—Widow Solley

Harvest Moon

In fields pregnant with pumpkins, we seven
women gather to hail the harvest, tossing seeds
and nuts like confetti, offerings for the titmice

and starlings, the catbirds and swallows
on their way down South. Bowls of muscadines
and gooseberries spill over for unpicky possums;

chunks of persimmon and pear tempt voles,
hares, and errant skunks. This ritual sharing,
a rebuke against winter's skeletal embrace,

reminds us to praise what is ever full: your grace,
the source of all holies, and soon, too, our bellies.
Under your maroon-gold gaze tonight,

there are apples to roast; ears of corn to pop;
pomegranate, quince, and huckleberry tarts to eat
by the hundredweight, when the dance of thanks is done.

"BLOW OUT YOUR CANDLES"

says Grannie B,
setting the carrot cake before Lulah,
mountainous at seven layers, and buried
billows deep in a Philly cream-cheese frosting—

her favorite. Vi's lemon chess pie waited
in the pie safe, but she wouldn't be home
for hours, and a birthday without Vi beside her
seemed about as festive as a case of collywobbles.

Something was off, and Lulah had known
it from the moment she woke. She said as much
to Vi as they dressed, but Vi pooh-poohed
alarms. Prattled about her date instead.

"Not another word about that pomaded viper
in your bosom! Bonham Ferry will *ruin* you!"
Lulah hollered as she stomped out the door.
Vi hadn't spoken to her for the rest of day—

and it had been so dreary, to have to miss
birthday customs over a snit: no racing
to (what's left of) the Colonel, no writing
dream letters to their future selves, no wearing

each other's clothes till Mama yelled go change,
no knocking off the afternoon to catch a matinee.
And now, to waste a wish on Vi's forgiveness—
with a bored-to-death breath, she blows out all eighteen.

Grannie hands her a knife and a stack of plates,
and Lulah cuts a small piece for herself, larger ones
for Grannie, Maggie, Wally, Mama, and the Widow.
The largest she places in the pie safe, an apology

for later. Lulah takes a bite, smiles in spite
of herself—such a cake could shake the blues
from a bolt of denim, a year of rainbows, a stack of '78s.
She feels a prick of sudden joy and sends

a prayer that this birthday finds Vi happy too,
but it's short-lived as a cake's delight:
separate from her twin, bitter worry
presses its fangs far too close to Lulah's breast.

As sunset clutches at the sky,
a blood moon rises over Caddo Lake.

Such a moon won't help tonight,
nor any spells: either his troth comes,
or truth—the return of her senses.
Vidalia buttons her sweater;
it's cool for early October,
and the rotting cypress stump beneath her is damp.
Four years of courting. He's nearly two hours late—

She sees him through the woods, then,
fixes a smile on lips too lately bitten
with worry. Oh, to be cursed
with faith in him as feeble as a spring faun,
that trembles before his vagrant heart.
As he climbs the path, shadows
of young pines cross his face like bars.

"You thought I wasn't coming,"
he accuses, not pausing to hand her
the tissue-wrapped baby's breath, toad lilies
he's brought, but pulling her down, pressing her close
like the blooms she's kept inside her journals,
one from each bouquet he'd given her.
She hears stems snap against her back,
wonders will there be a stain.

When he kisses her, she tastes stars—and gin.
"No—no, I knew you'd come."
She pulls away a shade too quickly, regrets
the way his jaw sets, how his embrace begins to crush,
and how, just as quickly, he thrusts
her away. "You'd never disappoint me
on my birthday," she pleads.

As if he remembers the lilies
still in his grasp, he tosses them at her;
lolling heads break off and scatter.

Maybe, she thinks, with tape and wire,
flowers can be salvaged, like this night—
there's still a chance he'll ask.
She finds her way back into wooden arms,
offers herself to him, tastes blood from his kisses.

The moon drains of color
as the dark of lake and sky converge.

ON THE THIRD DAY

Vi rises from her sickbed,
looking less like everlasting life
than everlasting death:
white as the sweet autumn clematis

Lulah has cut from the trellis
and set in a vase on her vanity,
her eyes thread-veined like the umbels
of the red spider lilies growing

by the creek. On the nightstand,
a Bible pushed aside makes room
for tea and toast and marmalade,
and a little scribbled rhyme:

> *Wake up, my sister, wake!*
> *Your shattered heart remake*
> *with the heart-glue of your twin:*
> *all my love is yours to take.*

Lulah, bless her, hoping tea
and verse can mend what magick
may not alter: time, time,
and the leaden weight of forfeit dreams.

Samhain

With prayers and chants and shadow words,
the veil to the Otherworld parts through:
sisters of our blood emerge!
Around this bonfire we converge,
O Sibley women, we summon you!

Come Helena once Blathnaid, and Urania
once Gormlaith, great mothers of the Gift
that made you flee your emerald home,
inscribe new secrets in this tome!
Come Mallaidh the Bitter, come Emer the Swift,

Máiréad the Pearl, Aigneis the Pure,
come Aideen, Lavena, and Flannery the Red!
See your daughters as we stand:
tonight we consecrate this land,
where the living and the dead

are one in harvest song—and will.
Your faces glow in fire's breath
while ours, in autumn moon and wind:
Goldonna, Maggie, Lulah, Vi, and
Lovette, Ida, Elizabeth.

> —We welcome from a darker realm
> you women wise, your magick ken!

> —And in this circle, turn we here,
> renew you for the coming year:

> *All Siobhlaith women, communion.*

BEST SERVED COLD

After church, I drop by Widow Solley's.
In her parlor, the tang of frankincense,
a breath of strawberry gone to rot.

Surrounded by silks and star charts,
charms, chimes, candles, cats (all black),
and a silver gazing ball, the Widow

peers through me, shakes her head. And *knows*.
"Revenge is sticky-tar magick, Lulah,"
but she leads me to her vegetable patch

out back. From among the vines,
she plucks a shiny squash
fat as her forearm, and offers it to me:

"Carve his name into the flesh, poke green
full of holes. Leave it in the icebox
till it blackens. On the waning gibbous moon,

bury what's left. Future loves
will find him feather-frail. Let this finish
it, and wish you no more for worse."

It's not the hex I had in mind,
but even not-quite-blood has its uses,
and will do well enough for now.

After

Though she has seen
Widow Solley's moonstone phial,   *Shame*
my sister says nothing   *does not*
of unexpected blood, of the cries

and gasps no fat pillow's feathers
could dull,   *wrap me*
as she tends my brow with a cloth,   *as tightly*
ties back my hair, a limp snake.

I will tell her
that the gnomon's shadow that crept   *as Grannie B's*
across Bonham's face   *knotted shawl*
did not tell his heart's time,

and Lulah will whisper to me kindness
and comfort, those flowered women.   *but I am cold*
But oh, the pale fellows   *as well water*
of wrath and retribution

array themselves in scarlet livery
in my sister's eyes. While I wait   *and twice*
out the wrenching of wild yam,   *as bitter*
the metallic taste of scheming on her tongue.

LETHE'S NOVENA

Widow Solley meets me at the barn door,
a blue-black beeswax candle in her left hand,
pencil and parchment in her right.
"Back again, Tallulah? Between you and Vi,
I've got egg money to spare."
The Widow doesn't spare a smile.

"She can't forget," I reply.
What I don't say:
that by night she sobs till tears etch grooves
in her cheeks, her eyes and nose red
as the geraniums Grannie B raises in her window boxes.

That she never eats,
and twice I've taken in her clothes,
unsure she's noticed,
even with my uncertain stitches.
That she's paler than dogwood blooms
by day, and restless as clouds before a storm.

The Widow knows this already.
"I have just the thing," she says, turning away,
the half-door shutting behind her with
an almost bat-like flap.

When she appears again, she carries
a pouch of powder, a jar of honey,
a copper bowl, bittersweet root,
and nine scraps of hand-made rose paper.
"The ritual is more important than belief,
Tallulah, since our Gift hesitates within you.
On a scrap, for nine nights, write:

> *What disquiets my sister's heart, erase;*
> *bring forth the ease of even days.*

Forget, forget the hidden face;
release all memory of love misplaced.

Nine times burn the paper in the brazier.
Nine times cast the ashes to the winds.
Nine times brew this poppy tea with honey;
make her drink it a shade before bedtime.
Nine times touch her head with bittersweet,
and tuck it beneath her pillow.

When her anguish
is as the filaments of an insect wing,
nine times smash the root beneath your heel.
Vidalia will be free.

But will you?
I fear the vengeance
that even now knots your veins
shall snare you longer than this lifetime.
I've something for that too, should you want it."

Nine times ninety lifetimes I'll hate
what's been done to Vi.
I take the Widow's magick with me,
leave coins in her hand.

Beaver Moon

Like a gash in the dam of night,
you flood the fields with a whitewater
rush of splendor, the sear grasses

that concede your weight bowing
and wave-like with November's
wheezing chill. The girl,

without coat and company—and thin,
so thin—strays into this current
as if to court the balm and counsel

you offer all such votaries. Before,
when she's come, she worked her Gift through you—
but prodigious tears and a flickering spirit

prevent petition tonight. You conjure
the creatures of light to her side,
let her drown in pelts of sudden sleep.

Supplication

My sister, her breathing
as regular as rows of cotton
on Highway 1, does not hear me
unlatch the window, shimmy
down the magnolia to our back yard.

Like the Widow Solley said to do,
I'm bare beneath my shift,
lift my arms to this new December moon,
call on Gréine, St. Monica, and Demeter.

Then I hold a smudge of sage
and juniper and light it, the scent
of Christmas, burning. The shadows cling;
no sticks crack beneath my feet
as I touch the smoldering roll
to the corners of our house,
scorch small ash-crosses on four shingles
to repel the shade of duplicitous love
that snares us Sibley women every time.

Beneath the gardenia hedge, leaves
black but glinting, I take out
a rosewood box, old treasures replaced
with seven strips of linen once red
now brown, which I've shredded
with fingers bare of rings
and stiff as sorrow. No shears
forged by man to defile this offering;
no spade but my hands to turn the earth,

which takes the cloth to heart,
transforms its purpose.
I drink the Widow's draft of wild yam,
black cohosh, faerie-wand, and pray.

Work my will, preparations;
what the Widow Solley said, be true:
all that was meant to hasten marriage
bring instead moon's flood;
what's false, cast out.

As the barred owl hoots its octave,
the pines tremble.

SISYPHUS

The woods give way to the barest lip of shore.
When Vidalia finally stops walking,
Honey sits beside her, the dog's pink tongue
long and impossibly shiny even in near-dark.

Vidalia has not brought herbs or spells or matches,
and December's moon, a hump-backed crone,
seems to chide the oversight. She does not need
those things tonight. The lake will do,

for this magick—to unbind a vine-choked heart,
set the vines adrift: four years of journal pages
torn free sink into the lake like swans that forget
to swim; pressed flowers from every bouquet—

thin, brittle—touch water and dissolve;
the palmetto brooch from her Sweet Sixteen
folds in on itself like a fortune and fades;
the green silk scarf lies upon the surface a moment

and is gone. She'd sink the heart if she could,
that, like a paper boat, sails on her tears and memories
but won't submerge. She turns her back
to the lake, calls Honey for the walk home.

Already, new vines begin to curl.

BEAN-SIDHE

Cutting behind Dixon's Dry on my way
to an after-dinner game in Princess Park,
I stoop to tie my shoe.

Beyond the crates and garbage
stacked high along the alley walls,
a laugh—*his* laugh—impales me
like a spike on the gates of Oakland Cemetery:

> *She wanted something special*
> *for her birthday. So I gave it to her.*
>
> *Oh, she fought me alright,*
> *that Irish catamount.*
> *Such fire in her you'd think*
> *she was her bitch twin!*

More laughter, his and someone else's.
I clap a hand over my mouth
too late to quell a cry. The ground sways.

> *—What was that?*
>
> *—Ain't nothin' but a cat in heat.*

And so the truth gores me like the Minotaur:
the blood, the candles, the spells
Vi cast and thought I didn't know about—
all those weeks afterward,
when she'd wandered wraith-like and weeping
till Grannie B brought her, limp as muslin,
to Highland, the gossips be damned.

He had done this to her, and I should have *known*—
known as if his infamy stained me as well,
and yet, I'd been too weak—

Vidalia, Vidalia,
I moan, keening for my sister,
for myself,
for what shall not be delayed for long.

One night soon, the banshee's cry.
One night soon, his death.

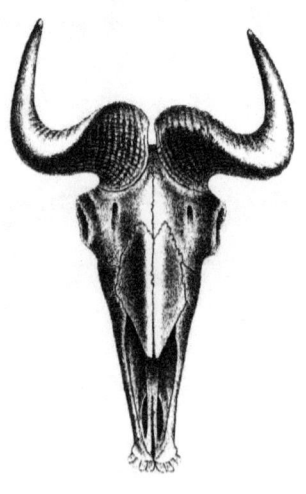

V.

Bring forth the arrowroot,
bring forth the obedience
from quince and scuppernong
boiled by hands
that have killed the place
of rock and dream.

—Widow Solley

Wolf Moon

There is howling tonight, Lulah,
long and sharp as fangs
that rip through the new year's

third darkness—and my soul,
a gray rabbit, escapes free on the wind
through the dormer. Shall I be chased,

cornered by the Black Mad Wolf?
The Others pace and snarl—and snap
at the rattle of keys as through bone and fur.

The White Army women, who bring
the draughts that dim Their hunting eyes,
whisper *A full moon stirs unrest—*

I cower in my warren for now,
where the Others must not find me.
The Black Wolf's jaws still tear the air.

Letter from Tallulah

Downtown Shreveport, February 1923

Today at Church, old Father Windbag
began with the proverb
"A merry heart does good like a medicine,
but a broken spirit dries the bones."
Believe me, there were a number of bones
drying in the pews by the time
he maundered through his homily. I myself
lost the will to live *at least* eight times,
and whispered as much to Wally
(when he wasn't snoring),
and didn't know anyone overheard me
till Good Christian Mrs. Crockett
said "Bless My Soul!" half a dozen times,
and Mama swatted me with her missal.
Meanwhile, Calvin and Magnolia
were making eye-promises for a little bit more
than peace be with you, and Mama didn't hit *them*.
Anyway, when I say Father ended with Lamentations,
I don't just mean the church goers'.
He wandered through six books of the Old Testament
like it was forty years in the desert.
And through it all, Grannie B behaved
as pious as a nun in black bombazine,
her head bowed over the Holy Book,
and looking for all the world
like she was following along, flipping pages,
moved often to say "Amen!",
even though ours ain't that kind of church.
And then I noticed it wasn't the Family Bible
at all, just the loose book cover she'd wrapped
around her old spell-and-remedy book,
which made me laugh, which made Mama
promise I'd be sorry when I got home—

and she didn't much like when I muttered
what's the point of grounding a fifty-year-old?
(Because that's how long it'll be till we leave.)
When Father *finally* gave the benediction,
people ran for the doors like Noah's flood
or maybe devil dogs were after them.
I bet the angels heard *"Deo gratias!"*
all the way in the clouds. So be glad
you weren't here, Vi. After a service like that,
no amount of prayer can save you.

—Come home soon, Lulah

Hunger Moon

To the north they name you for snow.
Here, others call you starving,
a stomach in a black, cold cavity,

that quivers with want—for Spring's
green blush, for bayous to jump banks,
for rabbits to bounce from warrens.

Those labels deceive: you are full
and warm as an unnursed udder
that craves a calf's curling tongue,

as I crave the Gift the White Army
lays siege to—they seize lavender
and sage she sends in a Valentine,

substitute unnatural sleep and physic,
spirit-bitter. Tonight I do not swallow
their famine moons, but suckle, gorge your light.

Letter from Vidalia

Highland Sanitarium, February 1923

Lulah—

Do you see the stars tonight,
like so many buttons on a great gray coat?
The Dove and Dog I see at once,
and then the Twins, Castor and Pollux,
on a long walk across the sky—
it makes me think of us, and I start
to cry, but I mustn't cry again—it's an art
the White Army stamps out, like the night's
with their pills—sarcasm like whiskey
under their breaths. (Thanks—the coat
you sent, its flowers orange as Pollux,
is warm as Honey-slobber.) All at once
the gas lamps surge in their sconces
and dim—the way houselights start
to flicker at intermission's end. All clocks
tell a lie it's ten, but it's eight at night
when they call bedtime, check petticoats
and pillows for anything sharp. (*Buttinskis*,
you would say.) A last glance at the sky
from my mouse-hole window, and I'm ensconced
between thin sheets and board—no sugarcoating
insomnia, I stay awake to startle
them, whisper to swan-fathers at night,
and then in day, speak of my sister Pollux—
but my mythology's wrong—Pollux
was my brother, I'll say—and they, in husky
tones *tsk-tsk* like metronomes, or censure me outright:
call for another sedative, like starburst, once
my fancy plays itself out, starts
to wrinkle in the chest, like an old coat—
the Colonel's moth-balled coat,

covered with dust and powder burns. Relax,
Lulah—I may be muddled, but my heart's
flight extends as the Dove in the sky,
lightyears and degrees, and only once
or twice, reaches an unhappy azimuth. Tonight,
as I draw your coat closer around me, the sky
like castor oil could drown you, Pollux, once
the stars, undone, reveal me, naked as the night.

—In madness (or not), "Lyssa"

Storm Moon

She shrugs out of the clouds
as one would a raincoat:
a bit clumsy, damp at the edges,

but on the whole untroubled
by the evening's downpour,
as if she's come for a late visit.

I have only some stale toast
to offer, and the cure-in-milk
Lecompte has left on the dresser.

Even the hungriest
could find little to eat here,
yet magick makes do with less.

I speak the words to coax
the thunder from my heart; a deluge
of light—company, but no answer.

Tossing the Gauntlet at the State Fair

Tallulah approaches the booth
just as he winds his pitch,
the fine cords of the poplin shirt
Vi made for him pulling taut
across biceps used to heavy lifting.

Beside him, a girl with painted lips
and a bodice too shocking to bear the name
clutches woolen teddy bears.
The carney snarls
behind his handlebar mustache
when milk cans go flying again.

"Had enough, Sonny?" he asks,
unhooking another bear from the wall,
and handing it to the girl.

"What do you think, Cora Pearl? Lucky seven?"
She giggles, a high-pitched whinny
that could make a gelding blush,
as he takes aim again.

Lulah aims as well,
her timing pitch-perfect,
stumbling straight into him
as he releases the ball,
sending it wild. The carney smirks.

"Sorry, Bonham! Don't know
how I missed seeing you
or the Cora of Babylon there."
Ignoring the girl's Theda Bara glare,
she offers to shake his hand.
He crosses his arms over his chest.

"Well, well, *Vidalia*, didn't know
they let you out of the loony bin already.
Getting a bit thick around the middle,
ain't you? Surprised your Mama
ain't scramblin' to find you a groom."
The girl titters but shoots Lulah
a look to curdle holy water.

"Why, I ain't no thicker around the middle
than your little *friend* here is,"
Tallulah says, playing along.
"Anyway, the cops figure
I can't find myself stuck
with some half-demon bastard
when the scoundrel didn't know
how to handle himself properly.
An amateur, they said. *A sheep pesterer.*"

He lunges at her then,
grabs for her throat. *"Why you little—"*
"See here!" the carney breaks in,
wielding a milk can above his head,
"I don't want no trouble!"
Tallulah doesn't back down.

Bonham, seething, shoves past,
pulls roughly at Cora Pearl's elbow.
Bears fall in a mound,
like a grave. He does not stop
to let her pick them up.

The carney hops from his perch,
gathers the abandoned bears,
and hangs them back up. He picks
up a baseball, looks hopefully at Lulah,
but she shakes her head.

Behind her as she walks
along the midway, she hears,
"3 Balls for a Nickel, 8 for a Dime!"

Tallulah on tenterhooks, biding her time.

Lenten Moon

The ground thaws, and nightcrawlers
clean house, leaving their burrows
to cast on the surface, where robins,

asleep by the time you rise,
flit fast to swallow them, to feed
their downy babies come the day.

Though you mark the last of winter's
occupation, you do not mourn
the fading chill; you are full

as a bowl of milk, as bayous after a squall,
as a repentant heart. You keep vigil
above this scene of small transformation,

worm into bird, that little prayer—
how it sustains you! Is it self-denial
to believe you'll not be gone by Son-rise?

CONTRABAND

The White Army had rummaged
through her cache again,
discovered Lulah's hankie
full of althaea and agrimony,
pine needles and plantain leaf,
sacrificed the lot to compost.

To cloak anything well in such a cell,
too small even for a proper chest—
even for sunlight, most days—
required more cunning
than she laid claim to,
and those women could out-sly
a skulk of foxes.

Vidalia half-smiled; the plantain leaf
was Lulah's little joke,
its power to thwart marauding hands
more superstition than truth.
But the others she'd have found use for,
to counterjinx the mutterings
of the frost-lipped nurses, stiff as meringues

in their uniforms, or to attract
the benevolent spirits
that surely, even here, in this sad refuge
on a hill, could ease the thoughts
of wayward reason, and scour hearts
like hers, petrified to stone,
till they gleamed.

Repast

So many hours
has she heard the starling sing
in the crepe myrtles.
This smudge on a cherub's pink cheeks
resisted her introductions—

but bread, the universal language,
coaxes even him,
though he keeps her at wing's length
while he pecks at the biscuit
she's saved from a breakfast
of thin grits and thinner eggs.

A week of meals she's shared—
his first to eat
while she remains close by.
The taming goes slowly.

She thinks of fair Branwen,
imprisoned three years
by husband Matholwch,
a queen made low to serve as cook,
flogged nightly, mistakenly,
for his disfigured horses—

Branwen who raised a starling
in the cover of a kneading trough,
taught it to speak, and to return
to the Island of the Mighty,
her letter of woe tied to its wing
that would usher in a brother's rescue:
a mountain and a wood
moving upon the sea—

and what came next,
a broken heart and death—
These are not the things to discuss
in polite company—not, certainly,
with this chary starling, this morning.

Though she has woe enough
for a thousand letters,
no such deliverance will come for her.

BEATITUDE

Purple drifts of myrtle blooms
plucked off by the squall
edge the muddy street as Lulah walks
the last few steps from Highland
to the trolley stop—

not one of their better visits,
with Vi so eked of spirit
she seemed translucent
as powdered milk and water
when Lulah gets proportions wrong.

Tales of new kittens could not rouse her,
nor a pocketful of rhymes
nor buttercups bundled
with juniper sprigs and faerie-wand,
to tide her through the next moon.
The kingdom of Heaven
may be Vi's one day, but no time soon—

Crackling on its wire,
the trolley stops before her and she boards.
As the driver rings the bell,
a rush of blossoms startles from the trees.

Visiting Day

Alone in the courtyard,
in the white gown and shawl
Grannie B crocheted for her,
Vidalia listens as the last
of "How Blest is He Whose Trespass"
warbles through the open atrium windows.

He is not blessed, she thinks,
not at all. She pushes her toe
against the dirt almost without thought,
setting the rusty swing she's in askew.

She does not care for company,
but it's the first Sunday in May,
and her sisters have written:
Magnolia, busy with wedding plans,
sends her regrets, but Lulah
promises to bring her chocolate
and new verses she's composed,
"though they ain't hardly any good."

In truth, Lulah's argus-eyes
are unwelcome. Her twin's sympathy
could scald the skin right off of her.
Better to breathe in the bustle
and prattling of Magnolia
and Grannie B and Mama,
consumed with somethings blue
and pennies in your shoe, too
busy to notice the quiet.

What Lulah doesn't say
is still too much.
In her white gown and shawl,
Vidalia closes in on herself

in preparation,
like a morning glory in the heat—
in the language of flowers,
love in vain.

Sympathetic Magick

Sitting together on the swing,
Lulah offers Vi a poppet,
certain the nurses won't suspect
its purpose and throw it out.

A crude thing, really, with buttons
for eyes, braids of yarn
almost their shade of red,
and a little stitched X for a mouth,
the doll is stuffed with belladonna,
bayberry, and St. Benedict's thistle:
to forget lost love, to purify and heal
the spirit, to protect against evil.

Those herbs the Widow suggested,
but Lulah has added sprig of pussy willow
to overcome grief, pine for strength,
and petals of peony, just in case—

Not that she believes Vi's gone mad—
though her last several letters
have hinted at strange tempers
and uneasy riddles,
revealed a wish to be renamed Lyssa—
but once a mooncalf, always a mooncalf,
and lunacy's never far off,
in a place like this.

Perhaps the doll will work its cure—
enough, at least, to persuade
the ghost-like doctors floating
beside Vi's bed to send her home.

She smiles as she slips
the doll in a pocket and begins a song

in a language that hovers somewhere
between the voices of flowers
and the timbre of wind.
Lulah joins in then,
in made-up words of her own—
      farrining-fa-folleree
      haddling-ha-ho

WALK A MILE IN VI'S SHOES

Tonight Lulah is passing—
at the music hall, if she missteps
as they dance to "Look for the Silver Lining,"
she pooh-poohs Bonham's puzzlement,
claims all the other dancers on the floor
make it too hard to move with him—
and wouldn't some fresh air be nice instead?

At the door, if she wills her blood
to warm, allows herself to be fluid in his arms,
she can bear his thick, fishlike tongue
when he forces his kiss upon her—
enough to pluck five pomaded hairs
with her own roving hand.

VI.

Where the vision narrows,
find the courage of the fig;
she who is lost
will never again renege.

—Widow Solley

FROM THE NORTH ACROSS THE LAKE, A MORNING WIND SNAPS THE LAUNDRY ON THE LINE LIKE SAILS SLIPPED OF THEIR RIGGING

The barn cats twine between
her ankles as she pins up another frock.
Sunlight spills too easily
through last night's lilac organdie—
just as well it's not her dress.

Some sheets, Grannie B's star quilt,
work shirts for Wally,
and she'll be done—plenty of time
left in the day to retreat to the hayloft,
where words against *him*
are sure to come, sharp as chicken wire,
as the stench of ammonia in an unmucked stall.

Between the two of them,
that man takes up too many
of their thoughts—a sister's regrets,
her own, a dark orbit
of nightshade-shimmered purposes.

A crow shrieks in the oak,
startling her and several cats.
Chance pays no attention,
and wanders underneath a shady hedge—
belladonna—
heavy with berries like black marbles,
to stretch and sleep—
a sign, if she needed one.

She finishes hanging the wash
before the sun reaches its apex,
rounds up the cats in the empty basket

(the ones that don't jump back out),
and carries them to the barn.

Inscriptions there are to craft today,
and magicks to ready for tonight's full moon.

Et Exuentes a Completorio

"It'll be alright, girl, it'll be alright.
My youngest son's run to fetch you some help."

His pointed face, black paint on weary night's
canvas, stabs into crows of dread. A yelp,

sudden, cur-like, and she retches blood. Tears
like stone petals fall—from her eyes, or his?

"Trol-ley?" wheezes Maggie, breath glue-thick—hears
"Naw, some drunken fool in a Caddie whiz

on by." Then this squawked plea: "Be *alright*, girl."
"She said—there'd be angels—in white—she said—"

"Ain't nothing like that. It's jest me, old Merle—
but I'll watch you till they come." On her head

his hasty crow kiss. What it is to die:
a Black man's solace, and a mother's lie.

COMING HOME

The White Army's attack:
I am not well enough to leave.
The men barrage me with warnings
like shells—

The first salvo booms.
She is too frail, her spirit a thread
the Fates could cut, claims one—
the kindest.

Another: *We're soon to break her,*
by God, of witchery's crutch.
He clutches a chart, black with notes,
like an Enfield, like Wally's.

The General, quiet, rounds, springs
forth in ambush: *She will lead*
a life of laudanum and lechery.
She must stay here!

"That all may be," says Grannie B;
her voice like cannon fire.
"but her sister lies dead,
and we need another mourner at the wake."

She signs a dozen pages—the armistice?
No—the White Army, heedless
of defeat, trails behind, shouting,
even as we storm the door, conquer the stairs.

Nor Altar Heap'd with Flowers

The silver aspergillum glints
with effort in the weary sunlight
as the priest shakes it at the casket,

holy water falling
into a bouquet of the grand magnolias
for which she was named,

still damp from morning's cloudburst.
Indolent on a bloom, a cabbage white
startles at the motion and flies off.

To think a week ago how she inscribed
cream vellum with sepia ink,
her practiced hand so even

in her letters, except at his name—
the extra flourish on the capitals
pure invention, like a flattened heart,

or to those with more exacting eyes,
the mistake of a pen allowed too long to rest.
And now to this: the white

of padded satin and painted wood—
the white of lace left hanging
in a mother's closet like an apparition,

the white, drawn faces of the assembly
like moons, brittle, on a black, black lake,
and, turned by grief, the white zero of Eros' heart.

On the Pier at Hawley Arm, Their Legs Hanging Over the Edge, the Sisters Watch a Storm Punch Its Way from the West

As the bruised clouds spread,
the air, thick and woolen all day,
shifts and trembles. The lake
blackens in response, while gators,

like logs, sink beneath the surface,
ripples vanishing almost instantly.
A pelican on a cypress stump
takes fright, takes flight, its white

feathers a momentary erasure
of the sky's embittered indigo.
The sisters ought to go in; a storm
like that can bludgeon a body with hail

faster than they can run the quarter-
mile to the house, but they know
what they will find there: broken hearts,
broken hearts, faded magnolias.

STRAWBERRY MOON

The statuary glints faience blue,
and the bronze Crucifixion above the priests
lost to Yellow Fever in 1873 glows

cold gold beneath you—but you are drawn
to the living: the young man, prostrate
on new grass, clutches her rosary

and her tintype—as still as any Catholic
here, now that his misery has spent itself,
a black cat shrunk to shadow.

Magnolias that edge the stone before him
lean in till one bloom falls, bejewels the hand
that holds the portrait. Maybe a trick of wind

or his sudden sigh or the residual magick
of a wedding day's lost love—or was it you,
set like a sixpence in the dark night's shoe?

LETTER FROM FR. BENTON SIBLEY WINNSBORO, S.J.

Manzanillo, Mexico, July 1923

Dearest Family—

Must I start with verses as is my duty?
Here, the words I have spoken to many
clothed in our sorrow: Paul says,
> *"We will not all sleep, but we will all be changed*
> *in a flash, in a twinkling of an eye,*
> *at the last trumpet. For the trumpet will sound,*
> *the dead will be raised imperishable . . .*
> *Where, O death, is your victory?*
> *Where, O death, is your sting?"*

I'll tell you where it is:
in this barren moon, my heart.
Oh, my dears, how are we to bear it?
How do we say goodbye to darling Maggie,
who was to be married this very June?

Can I say that she flies with angels now,
and believe it? Can I say we take comfort
that we shall to join her on the last day,
that we shall be one together in Christ?
Dare I say to you or to Calvin, her beloved,
that the Lord always has a plan for us,
and not cut my throat on religious saws?

Faith! The word is an obscenity;
I cannot be a priest in these matters,
but merely her loving brother, in pain.

—And yet, we must *trust* in the Resurrection.
We must have no doubt when Jesus tells us,
"She who believes in Me will live, even if she dies."

118

And she did believe!
She was righteous, even in her Gift!
And God knew as she left from Compline,
they were right with each other,
that it was safe to bring her to his fold.

I cannot say how we must move on,
my dears, only that we must—through prayer,
and perhaps through charms, and always through love.

—In Jesus's Name, Your Son and Brother, Benton

Grannie B's Lullaby

By twilight, mourners
and the merely dutiful have departed
Oakland for home, and I have come
to plant bulbs in Maggie's bit of earth
(well, and Cole's too, bless him,
gone these five years). *Not* magnolia;
the roots would riddle or smash
the graves before a decade's time—but daffodils.

Here, such flowers could not hope
to snare the foolish come spring,
but might be pleasant for some to see
on quiet walks and passing contemplation.
Three dozen for her, and two for him—
not that I loved him less, but it came
nearly to five dollars at Dixon's for the lot,
and he cut me a deal when I said who they were for.

I am sweaty down to my pantaloons
with the toil, and by the sixtieth bulb,
so encrusted with dirt I could pass
for a grave-crawler, were there someone
left in the park to scare. Already the Moon
takes her dais, and I bow despite my filth,
a quick but paltry homage, as I know
the family will wonder what keeps me.

Then a memory from childhood, and I sing—

> *Little baby,*
> *baby in the moonlight,*
> *moonlight, moonlight*
> *kiss you on the cheek*

Only baby,
baby with your eyes closed,
eyes closed, eyes closed,
till you're fast asleep

Moon shan't kiss you
if she sees you're peeking
peeking, peeking
Moon will turn away

Sleep now, baby
give yourself to dreaming,
dreaming, dreaming
Moon will stay.

Blood Moon

Red as Mars, and twice as warlike,
you smash through enemy lines—
the cracked loft doors—to march across

the hayloft like Sherman to the sea,
scorching straw bales, a battered plough,
a chicken or two. The sheets before me,

blank as midnight, halt your progress—
but feverish again, you flick at me
with shovels of fire, singe fingertips and soul

until they blister, until language bursts
free like a fox who cannot hear the bloodhounds
but feels them in the *thrum* of its pulse—

pages aflame with new verse, but at a cost—
Tonight a sacrifice will be made:
something hunted must fall, and blood be let.

CURSE

Where she has burnt away the scrub,
she draws a five-foot wide pentacle
in ash and dirt with two points
pointing north, the Sign of the Goat.

At each point, a new black beeswax
candle she lights in widdershins,
with tacks and needles and nails
at their bases to focus power—and his pain.

She takes the blade, purifies it in each
candle flame, then slices her left palm,
letting the blood drip into the star.
Its lines seem to ripple and stir.

She presses a cloth around the wound.
On parchment, she writes his full name,
lists his sins with cold purpose, the page wet
with ink tar black as his soul—and her rage.

> *May roaming eyes be crushed to powder,*
> *your forked tongue transform to sand,*
> *your fickle heart give way to cinders,*
> *that which makes you man, unmanned.*

> *May the darkest magick use me*
> *as I conjure forth this spell.*
> *May the devils find you worthy*
> *as I will you now to Hell.*

She rips the parchment in five pieces,
burns one at each candle, letting ash float
or fall at whim. Something of the forest
watches, watches, as if it wants

a clutch of demons to belch forth
from the pentacle. But there is only this *witch*,
as she blows the candles out deosil,
collects ash, sharpened metal, and strands

of captured hair in muslin pouches
she will bury at Hawley Arm,
at his home, the rail yard, and around town.
The star she leaves to do its work.

Blood Will Have Blood

I. *Leaving Union Station*

The Overnight to Kansas City,
a black sleeve on the starched shirt
of the station concourse,
is soon to board, but only a handful
of passengers idle on Platform Two.
Not quite nine, and already Bonham's
on his fourth shot of red-eye
in the Jefferson Hotel lobby across the street.

He wishes he could skip town—
the conductor'd probably pass him by
when he called for tickets—a perk
from working the yards—but he needs that job
to pay off the busted front end of the car.
No way to treat a lady, forcing her
to walk, when he wants to show her a good time.
Though Cora Pearl ain't no lady, he leers, not like—
He waves the thought aside, and slugs
down another shot behind the ferns.
He should go—
the desk clerk, moth-like and fluttery,
keeps trying to catch his eye.

The train whistle blows, impatient
as the tinny cornet solo in "Dippermouth Blues"
popping over the wireless. He stands,
gathers his jacket, and starts for the door
when *she* spins into the lobby—Vi, no, *Tallulah*—
red points on her handkerchief skirt,
wide as machete blades, flare straight out
from thighs nearly as creamy and lush
as her sister's. He watches as she sidles
up to the desk where she signs the register.
The clerk hands her a key.

Too late to sink back into the ferns—
she turns and fixes him with a stare
that licks at him like fire. The gas sconces dim.
As the space closes between them,
a mist—no, her perfume, leonine and predatory—
swirls around them, catches him by the throat.
"Let's get a drink," she says. "It's time we settle this."

II. *Blue Whale*

The back room at Blue's Apothecary
(everyone calls it the Blue Whale)
is crowded when they arrive,
so they cram into a table beside shelves
of bandages, bottles, remedies, and salves.
Lobo Sally sings "Sugartown Blues"
on an improvised stage of wooden crates,
the notes of the trombone and bass warring
for space in the smoke-heavy air.

> *You ain't gonna bring me down, boy.*
> *You ain't gonna bring me down.*

A waitress in a sapphire dress
with a V so deep across her chest
you could see to New Orleans
sets dark glasses down before they order:
moonshine, wood spirits—water—
for all Lulah cares. As she starts
to mince off, he turns to slip a bill
into the woman's bosom, misses
as Lulah adds a phial of wolfsbane, oleander,
poppy, tinctoria, belladonna powders,
and utters words lost to the cornet solo.

> *They said you was lying and cheating,*
> *Prowling beneath the moon like a hound.*

126

Oh my heart, it just wouldn't believe in
That—but you ain't gonna bring me down.

"Two Blue Screws," he says, and downs
both glasses, wincing as the booze burns
his throat—and his soul, maybe.
He motions to the waitress, two fingers.
She winks at him and hurries to the bar.
"What do you want, Lulah?" he asks,
squinting and rubbing his temples.
"I know what you did."
"*What* do you know?"

But he knows too:
he thinks of Vidalia, that night in the woods,
crushed like toad lilies beneath his lust—
of the Cadillac, the wash of blood
on the hood—the deer he hit—or Magnolia?

And then from his lips a desperate litany
bursts forth—so many sins
it's like Saturday afternoon at Holy Trinity
if confession was the blues:

the boozing, the brawling, the caterwauling
knock-down drag-outs,
thefts at work, fires he set, dirty deals,
the Bottoms whore he had to quiet
when she began to scream,
his hands squeezing, squeezing, squeezing—
Vidalia—how she crumpled, how she cried—
Magnolia's thud against the front end
loud as sacks of mail tossed off a rail car—

> *I ain't got no house to sleep in,*
> *My baby's long cold in the ground.*
> *There's no trains left to be leaving*
> *On—but you ain't gonna bring me down.*

He stops then, sudden, as if he knows
Lulah's tricked the words from him
with Sibley magick and unholy herbs.
He rubs his temple again, feels his throat
thick and wooden. The air in his lungs
congeals, cloying as syrup.
His face in the dimness has an indigo sheen.

      You ain't gonna bring me down, boy.
      You ain't gonna bring me down.

Lulah should be sick—anyone with a soul would be—
but she's cast her own to that other blue wail, ether,
with sacrifice and spells, trapped it in a loaf of bread
which she's hid inside a cask
and buried under Old Wives' Oak—
so that it might be untouched by what still must come.

"We need to get you out of here.
Why, you're not looking well at all."
His face contorts but he can't resist
as she pulls him to his feet
and leads him out.

No one notices as he stumbles and staggers
about the belly of the Blue Whale.
Just another drunk on a Saturday night,
and many others doing the same,
sway-dance-swaggering in time with the band.

      It won't take too much to get even.
      Soon you'll be seeing me around.
      A gun, a shot, and you'll be breathing
      No more—no more in Sugartown.

As they step into the alley, Lobo Sally's
throaty lyrics follow them into the evening
like no lover's promise ever.

III. *The Wages of Sin*

1.

At the end of the gravel road
behind the house at Hawley Arm,
Lulah stops the wagon. The horse whickers
as she hums "Who's Sorry Now?"
but the night otherwise is quiet.
Lulah jumps down from the seat,
unlatches the tail-gate,
and crawls onto the bed beside him.
He isn't moving, and when she presses
fingers to his throat, she finds
the herbs and fates have done her a kindness.
There's no reason to hurry, now.

Behind some bushes at the lake's edge,
where she'd brought the *Brittle Moon* aground
some days ago, she changes into an old shirt,
overalls, and boots. A newly-glinting axe,
some kerosene, hemp rope, and heavy stones
line the bottom of the boat.
She retrieves a garden cart, positions it
beside the wagon—

    Oh, Dark Mother, lend me strength!

rolls Bonham log-like into it,
and wheels him to the lake.

Inside the boat, she braces her legs
against the stern and pulls him
in on top of her. The oily stench
of pomade bites at her like a cottonmouth.
She scuttles from beneath him,
steps a shoe to the shore and pushes off.

A new moon makes a wall of lake and sky.
A thin fog above the surface droop-curls like ivy.
She paddles towards Tar Island Slough,
resolve the only light to guide her.
She sings, "Who's sad and blue? Who's crying too?
Just like *she* cried over you."

2.

The keel runs aground almost before she knows it.
She climbs out, peels off his seersucker suit
and the rest of his things as swiftly
as peeling a spud, glad for the darkness,
less for the worry of being seen
than having to confront a naked man—her first,
and not how she expected him.
She slips her arms beneath his armpits,
locks her grip across his broad, eely chest.
She staggers backward as she wrenches him
from the boat, his stiffening muscles
and rounded bottom pressed against her—
too close—as close to her in death
as he was to Vi in life. She drops him
in the ankle-deep water, then gathers tools.
The waves lap around him
with more peace than he deserves.

Disensouled, Lulah tastes no bile
in her throat, feels no metallic cold
antipathy to his unnatural exit,
her former passion bowed to focus.
And remorse, could it penetrate her purpose,
would disperse as a startled shade
as soon as she heaves the axe above her—

> Oh, Dark Mother, steady my hand!

and swings through shoulders, wrists, thighs, throat—
The head bounces away, an odd rabbit,
to lodge near a hollowed-out stump.

Blood, oozy like honey now,
beads the edge of the lake
or dissolves like guilt. She'll lash the sand
with a branch to mask the rest,
though no one's set foot on the island
in close to forty years. She takes rope
and knots limbs and head to stones
with net-like regularity,
and sets the departed back into the boat,
the only burial mound he's due.

There's just the trunk left—
not like any marble she'd seen
in a library art book, with its broken-off
limbs rubbed smooth with time.
His is too fleshy, still too soft.
She cuts into the chest with a boning knife,
fillets apart flaps of skin and tissue—

  Oh Dark Mother, stay my path!

then smashes the ribcage with a rock.
At the crack of bone, an owl hoots.

A slice, slice, slice through arteries,
and Lulah plunges her fist into his chest,
scoops out the heart. In her hand,
even with blood viscous and cool
trickling down her forearm, it menaces
no more than beef tongue in gravy,
or a sack of chicken livers.

Not the black stone you might expect.
Nor an empty cavity, after all.

Just a heart—one that surely never ached
from breaking each vow—which she dumps
into a pail in the *Brittle Moon's* prow.

3.

Inside the Sign of the Goat,
she digs a firepit, and deposits the trunk.
A wet body burns reluctantly;
she ought to have brought towels.
But kerosene makes short work of the lack—
a match, a blaze, a curse: it's done.
"You had your way, now you must pay,"
she sings, "I'm glad that you're sorry now."
Skin begins to crackle and hiss,
and muscles char, turn tough as tortoise shell.

She smears half a jar of mentholatum
beneath her nose, undresses,
and tosses clothes, hers and his, into the pyre.
She splashes a bit more kerosene on top,
waits a moment as the fires leap up,
then turns her naked body, arms lifted,
towards the hidden moon,

> *Oh Dark Mother, with this sacrifice,*
> *becalm one sister's psyche's ice,*
> *mend soon her heart and ease her grief.*
>
> *Conduct a second to paradise.*
> *And from the third, extract your price*
> *(if these do not a balance leave):*
>
> *what you will, will I suffice:*
> *handmaiden, demon, disciple, device.*

A thin crescent spears
the darkness, and extinguishes again.

4.

Heat, light, and time render fabric and flesh
to soot. Now to clean: water
to snuff what's left of the burning,
smoking bones shoveled into the boat.
Tools stowed, sand churned up
to remove stains and footprints;
pentacle annulled. A bath—

She leaves nothing behind that she can see,
and paddles the *Brittle Moon* back
into the slough, dropping bones
and weighted limbs at intervals,
which sink beneath the surface
with the softest of gurgles.

She pulls up to some reeds
just south of the pier at Hawley Arm,
fetches the pail with the heart,
then overturns the boat and its contents
into waist-deep water. Wading to shore,
pail in hand, she thanks the Dark Mother,
and whispers across the water,

> *Come, leviathans of depths opaque*
> *and slake your greed for carrion:*
> *may no eyes see what feast you make*
> *in mud and grass and slough and lake.*

That which fed on Sibleys
feeds the alligators now.

SCRY BYE BABY

In Widow Solley's parlor,
she and Grannie B stand before a pedestal
that holds up a copper basin, three-quarters full.
In their hearts, they already suspect—
the child's moon is off,
and shadows, nearly electric,
too long keep her company.
One sister's specter has become the other's.

Grannie B uncorks and overturns
a small philter, while the Widow chants:

> *May secrets sudden divest their guise;*
> *unbind the truth that moors in lies;*
> *what we fear to know, disclose:*
> *by this serpent make us wise.*

The serpent of india ink coils
through the water, and the Sign of the Goat
swirls into view, and then the letter *T*.

The Widow nods, but surprise,
like a rabbit, darts across Grannie's face.
No Sibley daughter had thought to work
a demon spell in nigh on two centuries.
For *this* daughter, who has spurned
the Gift at every turn, to find succor
in the Fiend could only mean—

"We have to find and break that star,
wash her clean in the Red's high tide—"
exclaims Grannie B.
"It's too late," says the Widow. "Look!"

In the basin, ink resolves
into a vague circle around a triad of dots.
Caput mortuum.

Unmaking at Old Wives' Oak

Fresh dark earth has been upturned
where a dozen would-be brides
have planted daffodils for spring.
Lulah can't help thinking of the bulbs
as little graves, and the women
as waiting for death in dupioni and lace.

But she's here to dig and plant as well,
and spares them no more thought
as she sets down her pail and finds
the star-marked knot in the trunk.
She sinks fingers into the dirt,
upsetting earthworms, pillbugs, beetles,
till she finds the cherry cask.

The bread inside is mealy and green-
dusty with mold. Lulah wrinkles
her nose, but a deal's a deal. She places
the loaf on a handkerchief, and empties
the pail into the cask.

It falls like an overripe alligator pear,
bruised and wrinkled and stinking
of burnt sugar and month-old possum.
After she reburies it, she prays

> *Oh, Dark Mother in ether's blue wail*
> *you've held my soul untormented.*
> *Take in exchange what's in this pail,*
> *a tattered heart to weight the scale.*
> *Restore my soul when I eat this bread—*

She gags it down and mutters thanks—
woozy and feverish, she begins to shake:
a lifetime of little sins, and unkind turns

and worser spites, sharp as when first erred,
besiege her at once, turn her hands bloody—
no stigmata, this. She licks them clean,
lone disciple at a dark communion.

Summer Portraits, 1924

Not all in the same picture now,
they are a collage of images on the mantle:

Padre Benton, in his cassock and sombrero
(not a *capello romano*), looms in front
of the doors to Santa María. Solemn
First Communicants flank either side
of him, their hands folded in prayer.
He looks towards where a man has left
his apple cart and burro beside the church,
must notice the one little Christ-bride
who offers the beast some fruit, the edge
of her mantilla catching on her arm
and blowing into the burro's mouth.

*

On the Courthouse steps, a dozen
new deputies stand together haphazardly,
as if the photo was struck before the men
were told to straighten up. The white stars
of their badges form an unknown
constellation in the disorder of their stance.
Hat brims pulled low over their eyes,
the men look stern, but indistinct,
except for Deputy Wally who tries
not to smile behind the brown mouse
of his moustache. Mayor Thomas
and Sherriff Hughes look on from the left.

*

Mama and Vi lounge on Grannie B's star quilt
spread out on the lawn. Kittens smudge
across the skirts of their wilting white

dresses. Mother and daughter are caught
mid-laugh, their features washed out
except for dark-tinged lips and penciled-in
brows, worn especially for the picture.
The sun's flattening effect makes them
similar as sisters, but Mama's hair spills
a ripple of silver from her crown.

*

Almost on the same spot of lawn,
Grannie B and Widow Solley crouch
together on cushions like two scrawny hens,
though the Widow's expression is hawkish;
years of knowing crease her dark face.
Fat braids pool at her waist,
black snakes asleep. Her left arm curls
around Grannie's shoulders, and Grannie
leans into the hug, though she holds
a lacy parasol at a strange angle for shade,
as if it's a prop she's been given to satisfy
the artist's eye. Too hot for bombazine today,
she wears a kind of gray habit with straight
sleeves cuffed at the wrist. An apron,
shapeless as a scapular, covers much
of the dress and hides her hands—
it's plain, even by nun standards. Nothing
about Grannie's smile is holy, though.
The two of them together can only mean
there's magick in the offing.

*

The last, of Lulah, is cut from the *Gumbo*
yearbook, but framed—taken in the reading room
of Hill Library. "Good luck on finals!"
is printed in italics at the top of an image
that shows academics at its most banal:

an undergrad peruses bookshelves
in the background; six more in front share
a study table—only one, besides Lulah,
a woman. A pot of devil's ivy peeps up
from books and notes stacked high.
Lulah, center left, wears puffed sleeves
and a pointed collar. She forms a vertex
to two young men in the foreground,
a cadet and the other, tweedy, rumpled—
a love triangle in the making. The three
seem unaware of each other, lost in study.

In photo black and white,
hinted only in her heart-shaped face,
what would come: love and blight and shadow.

VII.

Take rest beneath the taro's ears
that shuffle at the wind;
beware its salt that ushers in
a closing throat and stones.

—Widow Solley

THE HOUSE AT HAWLEY ARM

At the house at Hawley Arm
boarded up these twenty years,
all the ghosts have floated on
toward less desolate frontiers:

homes where mullioned windows
hang crack-free behind their dust,
where doors, sagging here in jambs,
don't flap and slam upon a gust.

Such things ought not concern
a ghost, who never feels the cold,
nor meets a door impenetrable
to ether, dank, or mold—

but still it wants for company,
each lonely apparition.
A haunting with no one to haunt
is a dispiriting position.

And so the house at Hawley Arm
lies vacant of its ghosts:
the Sibleys who lived there once,
the Sibleys once their hosts.

CAST OF INVENTED CHARACTERS

Major:

BONHAM FERRY (1901-1924), an oily villain and beau of Vidalia.

IDA SIBLEY LEBOEUF SIBLEY ("Grannie B," 1852-1938), grandmother to the Sibley Winnsboros, mother of Goldonna and six other children, and distant cousin to Minden Sibley, whom she married in 1871 (hence the double Sibleys in her name). Because she has Sibley blood on both sides, she is profoundly gifted in magicks.

MAGNOLIA SIBLEY WINNSBORO ("Maggie," 1899-1924), eldest sister, good with magicks; she was engaged to Calvin Eros at her death.

TALLULAH SIBLEY WINNSBORO (b. 9:06 a.m., October 1904), the younger twin, a reader and writer, and less successful with magicks.

VIDALIA SIBLEY WINNSBORO (b. 8:58 a.m., October 1904), the elder twin, and good with magicks.

WIDOW SOLLEY (Rodessa Zylks Solley, 1853-1939), a distant cousin of Grannie B by marriage, and Grannie B's best friend. Like Grannie B, she is profoundly gifted in magicks.

Minor:

CORA PEARL, a strumpet.

MRS. FLORIEN CROCKETT, a lady of society and gossip.

MR. DIXON, an owner of a dry goods store.

FR. BENTON SIBLEY WINNSBORO (1898-1985), the eldest brother, and a Jesuit missionary priest in Manzanillo, Mexico.

COLE SIBLEY WINNSBORO (1905-1918), the youngest brother who dies when he falls out of a tree.

GOLDONNA SIBLEY WINNSBORO ("Mama," "Goldie," 1875-1936), mother of six, who married Delhi Winnsboro (1870-1916) in 1895.

STONEWALL SIBLEY WINNSBORO ("Wally," 1900-1972), the middle brother who fought in World War I.

Others Named in the text:

AIGNEIS THE PURE, a descendant of Helena.

AIDEEN, sister to Máiréad the Pearl, and descendant of Helena.

CAVETT WINNSBORO, brother to Mama's husband.

CHANCE ("Cloudy with a Chance"), a kitten and Tallulah's familiar.

THE COLONEL, a magnolia tree named after Grannie B's father, Col. Clarence Sibley LeBoeuf.

DELHI WINNSBORO, Mama's good-for-nothing husband who falls off a bridge.

ELIZABETH, daughter of Grannie B, and sister to Mama (Goldonna).

EMER THE SWIFT, a descendant of Helena.

FIGARO ("Figgy"), a barn cat.

FLANNERY THE RED, granddaughter of Urania.

HELENA ONCE BLATHNAID, the original Sibley foremother, and twin of Urania once Gormlaith.

HONEY, a dog that Vidalia rescues.

LARASUE BUCKELEW, a pregnant soon-to-be bride and subject of gossip.

LAVENA, granddaughter of Urania.

LECOMPTE, a nurse at the Highland Sanitarium.

LOBO SALLY, a blues singer in the Blue Whale speakeasy.

LOVETTE, Grannie B's older sister, and descendant of Urania.

LYSSA, a name Vidalia gives herself in correspondence while in Highland Sanitarium.

MALLIADH THE BITTER, a descendant of Urania.

MÁIRÉAD THE PEARL, a descendant of Helena.

MERLE, a man who watches over Maggie as she dies.

OLD PAPI, an aged Confederate soldier who hangs out in front of Dixon's Dry Goods.

ROSMERTA, a cat and Mama's familiar.

URANIA ONCE GORMLAITH, the original Sibley foremother, and twin of Helena.

Notes on the Poems

"The Three Hour Siege at the Caddo Parish Jail"
Caddo Parish, Louisiana holds the infamous distinction of recording the second highest number of lynchings in the United States from 1877-1950. (*See* "Map of 73 Years of Lynchings." *New York Times. NYTimes.com.* 9 Feb 2015. Web. 27 Sept. 2015.) This poem refers to a three hour attack on the Caddo Parish jail, where a "mob of 1,000 men and boys" sawed through the walls of the jail and dragged Ed Hamilton (also known as Edward or Earl) from his cell and hanged and murdered him for suspicion of "attacking a ten-year old white girl." (*See* "Louisiana Negro Lynched: Mob Hangs Little Girl's Assailant While Guardsmen Are Assembling." *New York Times,* 13 May 1914. *NYTimes.com.* Web. 9 March 2014.)

"Grannie B Tells the Origin of the Mounds"
The Mounds were piles of earth, often exceedingly large, that appeared over the Upland Flats of Louisiana and throughout Arkansas and Texas. A number of theories posited their existence, from a "race of giants," to ants, wind, pressure, and "aqueous volcanoes." (*See* O'Pry, Maude Hearn. *Chronicles of Shreveport.* Shreveport: Journal Printing Company, 1928.)

"Vidalia Casts for a Soul Mate"
This poem takes its structure from typical love magick spellcasting, which focuses the practitioner (or witch) on three specific actions: visualizing the qualities of the intended loved one, collecting the tools of magick which will aid in spell performance, and recognizing the Goddess as the source of power.

"The Colonel's Last Stand"
The Battle of Mansfield, part of the Red River Campaign in the Civil War, took place on April 8, 1864. Led by Gen. Nathaniel P. Banks, Union troops attempted to capture Shreveport, then capital of Louisiana, but were turned back by Major Gen. Richard Taylor. Union troops retreated to Alexandria at the defeat. (*See* "Mansfield." *The Civil War Trust,* n.d. *CivilWar.org.* Web. 12 Dec. 2014.)

"The Four Horsemen of the Apocalypse"
Besides being a biblical reference to Revelation 6:1-8, *The Four Horsemen of the Apocalypse* is a 1921 silent movie produced by Metro Pictures that starred Valentino, and was based on a Spanish novel of the same name by Vincent Blasko Ibáñez.

"Spring Training"
Exhibition games were often played between Major League baseball teams like Babe Ruth's New York Yankees, and "farm league" teams like the Shreveport Gassers. In the beginning of March 1921, the Yankees arrived in Shreveport for a month of spring training, which included playing a series of games against the Texas League Gassers. In one particular game on May 12, 1921, Babe Ruth played especially poorly, due in part to injuries and in part to a soggy field, disappointing Shreveport crowds. (*See* "Ruth Flails Air, But Yankees Win: New Yorkers Defeat Shreveport in First Nine-Inning Game by Score of 7 to 3." *New York Times*, 13 March, 1921. *NYTimes.com*. Web. 6 Nov. 2012.)

"Familiar"
Michael Robartes and the Dancer is a 1921 book of poetry by William Butler Yeats, among whose famous poems include "Easter 1916," "A Prayer for My Daughter," and "The Second Coming." This poem playfully riffs on lines from "The Second Coming."

"The Invisible Empire on Parade"
The presence of the Ku Klux Klan (the "Invisible Empire") in Louisiana dates from 1921, and the city of Shreveport became Klan headquarters for the state. Historian W. Chris Hale writes that the KKK in Louisiana was initially "unconcerned with the national aims of the Ku Klux Klan" (including "immigration, the Jewish problem, or white supremacy"), fancying itself instead as a kind of vice squad, policing all manner of moral improprieties, no matter the race. Additionally, owing to the overwhelming number of white Protestant Christians living in Shreveport joining the Klan, the Klan directed intense religious intolerance towards Catholics. Hale continues, "Klansmen . . . carried and distributed 'Do You Know' cards. These cards listed fifteen assertions essentially claiming the pope was a

political autocrat, hell-bent on dominating the government of the United States." (*See* Hale, W. Chris. "The Ku Klux Klan in Northwest Louisiana." *Wicked Shreveport*. Charleston, SC: The History Press, 2012. 33-45. Print.)

"Loaded Down with Sugar and Rice for Mama and Quilting Swatches for Vi, I Run Smack Dab into That Unctuous Bonham Ferry"
The last two lines of this poem are a corruption of lines from Tennyson's *Sea Dreams*: "…but gifts of grace he forged,/ And snakelike slimed his victim ere he gorged;".

"ERA at the WDC"
As women began to mobilize for a constitutional amendment—Equal Rights for All—and for a National Women's Party, organizations like Shreveport's Women's Department Club, founded in 1919, became a safe haven for women to debate women's issues and women's suffrage. While the poem mentions that it's a full year after national ratification before Louisiana recognizes women's right to vote, Pamela Tyler at the University of Southern Mississippi writes, "Louisiana lawmakers did not make their peace with the reality of the women suffrage amendment until 1970, when at last they ratified the measure in a symbolic acceptance of the fifty-year reality of votes for women." (*See* Tyler, Pamela. "Women Suffrage." *KnowLA Encyclopedia of Louisiana*. Ed. David Johnson. Louisiana Endowment for the Humanities, 4 Feb. 2011. Web. 5 May 2014.) Samuel Gompers, President of the American Federation of Labor, opposed equal rights, on the grounds that employers would remove safety measures designed for women's protection in industry. Both Gompers' protest and a reference to John D. Williamson, a Shreveport lawyer who endorsed Equal Rights, appear in the article "Plan Equal Rights Campaign in the South: Women's Party to Seek Enactment in Seven States—Gompers Renews Criticism." *New York Times*, 16 Jan. 1922. *NYTimes.com*. Web. 8 March 2013. (A week later, a reprint of Gompers' protest would appear in "Gompers Says Strict Equality is Dangerous: Purpose Praiseworthy of Removing Legal Inequalities from Women, But Actual Effect Would be Damaging." *The*

Garment Worker: The Official Journal of the Garment Workers of America, 27 January, 1922. Vol. 23, No. 15. p. 6. Print.)

"Bean-sidhe"
Bean-sidhe, which translates to "woman of the hills" is the Irish spelling of "banshee." (*See* Lindemens, Micha F. "Bean-Sidhe." *Encyclopedia Mythica,* n.d. *Pantheon.org.* Web. 9 March 2011.) This poem uses this spelling to pay tribute to Irish folklore and the Sibley sisters' Irish heritage.

"Samhain"
The names listed in this poem refer to the Sibley genealogy of witches, with Helena (Blathnaid) and Urania (Gormlaith) being twins from the 18th century who fled Ireland and came to Louisiana to practice their Gift.

"Repast"
The Mabinogion, 12th-13th century Celtic literature, relays the story of Branwen, sister to Bendigeidfran a British king, who is unhappily married to the King of Ireland, Matholwych. She is forced to serve as a slave. In the folklore, she tames a starling to fly to her brother and beg for rescue. Bendigeidfran sets across the Irish sea with his forces, and Mathlowych attempts to avert war by making his son by Branwen king. When her son becomes king of Ireland, he is killed, which provokes a war that only a handful of Irish and Welsh survive. Branwen dies from a broken heart at the destruction of both peoples. (*See* Davies, Sioned, trans. *The Mabinogion.* New York: Oxford UP, 2007. Print.)

"*Et Exuentes a Completorio*"
Compline is the last church office of the day, and this Latin phrase, deriving from the Rule of St. Benedict, translates to ". . . and, after leaving Compline . . ." Here, after leaving Compline, Maggie is a victim of Bonham's hit-and-run.

"Nor Altar Heap'd with Flowers"
The title of this poem borrows from a line from John Keats' "Ode to Psyche."

"Letter from Fr. Benton Sibley Winnsboro, S.J."
This quotation from Paul appears in 1 Corinthians 15:51-55. The adapted quotation from Jesus appears in John 11:25.

"Blood Will Have Blood"
This poem takes its title from a line from Shakespeare's *MacBeth*, Act III, Scene 4, line 129. Additionally, the poem borrows several lines from "Who's Sorry Now?" a 1923 song written by Ted Snyder, Bert Kalmar, and Harry Ruby. The song was later a hit for Connie Francis, and the subject of a copyright lawsuit. (*See* Gilliam, Annette. "Copyright: Who's Sorry Now?" *Loyola of Los Angeles Entertainment Law Review*. Vol. 6: 1986, 125-145. Print.)

About the Author

A Louisiana writer living in Atlanta, Georgia, **JC Reilly** writes across genres and has received Pushcart and Wigleaf nominations for her work, as well as awards from the National Federation of State Poetry Societies, the Georgia Poetry Society, and the Louisiana Division of the Arts. She is the author of the chapbook *La Petite Mort* and a contributing author to an anthology of occasional verse, *On Occasion: Four Poets, One Year*. Follow her @aishatonu.

www.ingramcontent.com/pod-product-compliance
Lightning Source LLC
Chambersburg PA
CBHW031958010726
47493CB00007B/2256